Iꙅɴiꞇed By Flames

Hidden Realms of Silver Lake
Book 6

Vella Day

Sometimes even a dragon shifter can't catch a break.

While Blake Masters is elated he's found his mate, convincing Greer Caspian that they are destined for each other is another matter. Between dealing with his now ex-girlfriend to battling an evil that seems to have many faces, there's never enough time to explore the depths of his desire for her.

Fate's timing couldn't get any worse. Just when Greer is ready to admit that Blake and she belong together, some strange transforming werewolf from Earth breaks into her house and robs her.

They decide the only way for any peace and quiet is to go after this guy. Two dragons against one wolf? It's sure to be a slam dunk. Right? Too bad she ends up traumatized once more and is forced to put her relationship with Blake on hold.

What will they have to do to find the time for the important things in life? Like mating.

Chapter One

"YOU'RE FREE TO go," Detective Caspian said as he unlocked the cell door and motioned Blake Masters out.

Thank goddess he was free. Blake never wanted to step foot in another cell again. He swung around to face the detective. "Don't get me wrong, I'm thrilled to be out of there, but may I ask why you're letting me go without a trial?"

He had been accused of kidnapping a woman who worked at SinCas jewelers. They'd even shown him the security footage of him injecting one of the employees with something and then carrying her lifeless body to a warehouse where he'd promptly passed out. Clearly, he was guilty. The problem was he remembered none of it.

"We needed some time to investigate not only the kidnapping but the murder in the warehouse. The evidence points to the fact that you were not, shall we say, of sound mind at the time. Greer Caspian, the woman you abducted, vouches you didn't kill the man who came into the warehouse."

Even though relief was racing through every cell in his body, Blake was almost more surprised to learn that Greer was a Caspian. He'd had no idea she was someone who came from such a well-connected family. Most of the time, wealthy people commented on that fact. She had not.

He was also thrilled that her family hadn't dumped him in a deep hole and forgotten about him. "I'm thankful for that. To be honest, I thought Greer would want my head on a platter."

"Both she and I are well aware of the dark entity and what he is capable of. After examining the marks on the warehouse body, it was evident that this entity killed the man, not you. Greer mentioned the multiple marks on your body, so we are sure you were not responsible for drugging my cousin either. The dark entity made you do those things."

"Thank you for being so thorough and not jumping to conclusions." If the police hadn't been, he might never have seen the light of day.

"It's our job."

Good to know. From what little Greer and her family had told him before he was taken into custody, this entity had killed all of its other victims. Blake was the first to survive.

"Where is this entity now?" he asked.

"He's dead, thanks to Angelique Carson and Thane Sinclair."

From his tone, that was all the information Blake was going to get, though it meant he'd never learn why he'd been spared. "I'm glad."

"So are we. Crystal Willows is waiting for you in the lobby."

The expected rush of excitement didn't surface. That was strange. "Thanks for calling my girlfriend."

"Of course."

When Blake walked into the lobby, Crystal was seated with her hands knotted in front of her. Her eyes were slightly bloodshot as if she'd been crying, and her shoulders sagged, but she still looked beautiful to him.

Crystal looked up, smiled, and then raced toward him. She threw herself into his embrace. "Are you okay? I don't understand why they arrested you."

Originally, when he'd been escorted to the station, Blake had been allowed one phone call, and that call had been to his lawyer buddy, Steve. He'd asked him to call Crystal about the arrest but not to give her too many details. She'd only worry more.

"We probably shouldn't be discussing this in the station," Blake said under his breath. "Let's get out of here, and I'll tell you everything. First though, I need to shower. Being in a cell for two days was gross."

Crystal threaded her arm through his. "I can't imagine what you went through, but I'm glad they released you."

"Yeah, me too." The two days in jail had given him time to think, and Crystal wasn't going to like what he had to say.

Blake had met Crystal when she came to work as a teller in the bank he managed, and he'd been instantly taken by her sweet nature. Because she was a tiny, take charge brunette with a killer body, he'd asked her out the first week. She'd accepted, and the rest was history.

Being a dragon shifter, he should have waited for his mate before dating someone, but after a hundred years, he was tired of being on edge, always wondering if she'd ever appear. It got to the point where he wasn't sure if mates even existed—at least not until he had met Greer. It was unfortunate that he hadn't met her under better circumstances—like before he'd kidnapped her and all. Now, she might not give him a chance to see if they had a future.

When he'd been almost mortally wounded, Greer had helped heal him. That was when his whole body had come to life for the first time.

It was possible that because the dark entity Greer referred to as Mange had taken over his body that it had tainted his response to her. He'd been hoping that when he saw Crystal again his old feelings for her would surface. But they hadn't.

He'd dropped a hint about wanting to marry Crystal, but now he wasn't so sure. His indecision had run rampant when he was in jail. He couldn't just break up with Crystal though without knowing for sure whether he and Greer were meant to be together. While dating for six months wasn't a real long time, being with Crystal had become comfortable—so much so that he thought it might be time to make it permanent.

If he and Crystal did split, it would devastate her. The poor woman had more or less been abandoned as a teenager when her dad had killed her mom when Crystal was only seventeen. Thankfully, once her father had been imprisoned, she went to college and never looked back.

He felt terrible that Crystal, a human, looked up to Blake as her hero. If only he could be sure she'd move on if he told her he wasn't ready to settle down with her—now or ever—Blake would approach Greer faster than water evaporated on a hot day.

"Did they feed you okay?" Crystal asked with such sincerity his guilt surfaced once more.

It took a moment to focus on her question. "The food was okay. I was still healing from everything so I really didn't care what they gave me."

She wrapped an arm around his waist and led him to her car, acting as if he were an invalid. He slid into the passenger seat while she walked around to the other side. "Do you want to go to your place or mine?" she asked with such innocence.

The way she said it implied she believed he'd want to make love with her, which was a reasonable assumption. While he had been injured, he had healed. "My place. As I said, I have to shower."

He adored Crystal, but after what just happened, he wasn't about to run down to the jewelry store and buy that ring—not when his dreams had been filled with Greer's face. The whole thing was absurd though. He and Crystal were perfect for each other. They were both into finance, both loved to run in the mornings, and they each really enjoyed seafood. It was a perfect match—or so he believed until he'd met Greer.

Then everything in his life turned upside down. For now, he'd pretend—or sort of pretend—that everything was back to normal with Crystal. Before he told her he wanted to reevaluate things, he needed to see Greer again. If nothing else, he had to make sure she really was his mate. Now healthy, his dragon would let him know if they were fated for each other.

"Steve told me that something took over your body?"

"Yes."

"I can't even imagine what that was like." Crystal fired up the engine and pulled onto the road once the traffic cleared.

Blake really didn't want to talk about those few hours, but Crystal deserved to know. He'd just leave out why he was in the jewelry store in the first place. "All I felt was a slight pain at first, followed by a mind-blowing explosion in my brain. Then nothing. It was as if I didn't exist while this thing was inside me. The next thing I remember was waking up on the floor of a warehouse. I hurt everywhere. Apparently, I had burn marks on my chest, my back, and my arms. But don't worry, I'm good now."

"Oh my heavens. I'm so glad you survived. Did this person shoot fire at you?"

"No. If it had, I would have shifted to protect myself. According to the woman I kidnapped, the injuries were due to some dark entity leaving my body. The cops have seen this kind of exit wound before. From what they have figured out, the entity took over all of my thought processes and made me do things I never would have done on my own. When it left my body, instead of exiting in one spot, it left in multiple places, which is why I lived." Or at least that was the working theory.

"I am so sorry this happened to you." She reached over and squeezed his leg. "Where is this entity now?"

"He's dead."

Her shoulders relaxed. "Oh, thank goodness."

They said little until they arrived at his place. He needed some time to himself, even though he understood Crystal wanted to be with him. After all, she'd almost lost him.

When she pulled into the parking lot behind the bank, he turned to her. "I'm going to shower and then take a nap. I hope you don't mind. I haven't really slept in a few days."

She placed a hand on his arm. "Of course not. You should rest, but how about if I come over later and cook you some dinner?"

Crystal looked so hopeful that he didn't have the heart to tell her no—but he had to. "Could I have a rain check?"

Her gaze lowered. "Sure."

Blake's heart broke seeing her like this. "Tomorrow night I'll take you out to dinner. How's that? I'm sure you would enjoy a break from cooking."

"If that's what you want, sure. Call me, okay?"

"I will." He leaned over and kissed her, hoping for that rush of excitement that always came when they were together. While the contact was pleasant, it wasn't what it had been before. Maybe it was the trauma of being possessed, arrested, and then stuffed in a nasty jail cell that affected his psyche.

"Get some rest," she said.

"I plan to."

As soon as he jogged up the steps to his condo on top of the bank, a sense of freedom surrounded him. Jail had sucked, and he never wanted to return. Closure however would never completely come, because he would never learn why he had been targeted. All he'd done was enter a jewelry store to buy a ring for Crystal and ended up almost dying. The only positive—for him but not for Crystal—was that he'd met Greer. It was possible that she would tell him he was full of shit, and that they weren't mates after all, but he owed it to himself to see if they were.

Damn, he knew nothing about the enigmatic woman other than she worked in a jewelry store and was from one of the most prominent families in all of Tarradon. For all he knew, she was already mated to someone else.

Crap. Blake headed to the shower, hoping the hot water would clear his head.

"YOU SHOULD BE resting," Tory Sinclair told Greer as she added a pair of sardonyx earrings to the display selection.

Greer stashed her purse under the counter and grabbed the polishing cloth to clean some smudges off the glass display. Her cousin was so protective, but Greer knew what she needed. "I can't rest. I need to be working."

"I know the sedative has worn off, but what about the emotional trauma? You seem a bit off. Distracted perhaps."

"I just walked in. How can you tell?" Greer waved the cloth and then set it down. Tory had a sixth sense about things. "You're right. I am off, and it's not physical as much as mental."

Even though there weren't any customers in the store, Greer really didn't want to hear what her cousin would say when she told her what, or rather who, she'd been dreaming about. Tory was a take-the-bull-by-the-horns type of woman. Knowing her, she'd say to march over to the bank and ask Blake out. If they were mates then she needed to find out now. To hell with his potential fiancée. Greer however possessed a bit more finesse than that.

Tory leaned against the counter, her brows pinched. "Did you have a nightmare or something?"

"No. Surprisingly, this has nothing to do with the dark entity and everything to do with Blake." Crap. She hadn't meant to blurt that out.

"The man who stabbed you with the needle and then kidnapped you?"

"Yes." She would have a hard time articulating what she felt, mostly because she was confused by it herself. "Did Anderson say what kind of guy Blake was?"

While he seemed nice, he could be some thug for all she knew. So what if he worked at the local bank? Their cousin, Anderson, had been in charge of the investigation, so he would have done a deep dive on the guy.

Tory shrugged. "Just that he manages the bank down the street."

"He told me that much." The last thing she remembered before the incident was Blake walking into the store and asking about an engagement ring. That meant those weird, albeit rather erotic pulses she'd felt when she first touched him must have been a result of the trauma of being sedated and then kidnapped and not because he was her mate. Darn.

Yes, he is, her dragon finally said.

Now she talks? Her animal had been silent all night when she needed answers the most.

"Did Anderson say anything else about him?" Greer asked as innocently as possible.

Tory placed a hand on her arm. "Why the interest? You said you didn't believe he was responsible for what happened."

"I don't."

"Why does it matter who he is?"

Greer normally kept things to herself, but she needed advice. So what if her cousin didn't have a mate of her own. Tory was a good judge of character. "This is going to sound really weird, but when I was in the cage and first saw Blake on the floor, the moment I touched him, a kind of excitement raced through me."

"Excitement? As in lust?" Tory's eyes widened.

She wished her cousin didn't act so surprised. "I'm afraid so."

"Since you told me he came into the store to buy an engagement ring, surely you aren't thinking there could be something between you, are you?"

Okay, it did sound lame. "I guess not. I should just move on, but I can't stop thinking about him."

Tory placed a hand on Greer's arm. "Greer? Are you thinking he's your mate?"

When she said it like that, perhaps it had been wishful thinking. Oh, sure, Greer acted like the perfect businesswoman, always putting her job first, but deep in her heart, she longed for a family of her own. "I don't know what to think."

Tory lowered her hand. "Then you need to find out!"

Just as she made that announcement, the doorbell to the store rang. When Greer looked up, her heart jerked.

Tory checked out the newcomer, looked back at Greer, and then tossed her a sly smile. "Lookie, lookie. Why if it isn't Mr. Blake Masters," she said under her breath.

Greer's stomach tumbled. Her cousin had seen the security footage and knew who he was. The big question was whether he was here to buy that ring or speak to her.

Chapter Two

B LAKE WASN'T SURE if it was a good idea to visit Greer or not, but if he didn't, he'd never know if his imagination was playing tricks on him. Just because she wasn't demanding he rot in jail for what he did—dark entity or not—didn't mean she liked him. Hell, he wouldn't be so quick to forgive someone if that person had kidnapped him. It didn't matter that Blake had no will of his own at the time.

Then there was Crystal—the woman he had previously believed he wanted to marry. It was possible that the trauma had messed with his head and was making him doubt himself. Men got cold feet all the time, right?

No, you idiot. Greer is your mate, his dragon grunted.

You might be right. Blake was so confused he wasn't sure if the swirling emotions inside him were ones of joy or depression.

It was time to find out which one. As he stood in front of the jewelry store, he wasn't even sure if Greer worked today until he spotted her near the back, dressed in a classy blue and white polka-dot dress wearing red heels—the same red heels she had on when he'd taken her.

Blake inhaled and pressed the button. A blonde woman un-locked the door and smiled as he entered.

"May I help you?"

"I'd like to speak with Greer."

Her grin widened, but he didn't dare try to figure out what that meant.

When Greer and he locked gazes, his dragon scratched and

clawed. Had he not been wearing a long sleeve shirt, his black scales would have been flashing against his mostly sand colored ones. He had no doubt his dark brown eyes must already have teal-colored swirls running through them.

Are you finally convinced she's your mate? his dragon asked.

I'm still unsure.

For real? Look at her, dude. Her eyes couldn't get any more purple. And check out those light-yellow scales flashing under her skin. What more proof do you need?

I don't know, Blake shot back, almost afraid to have his dream of finding a mate come true.

Just because their dragons seemed to be interested in each other didn't mean Greer the woman would desire him.

"I see you were released," Greer said as she approached him.

"Yes. All charges were dropped. I'm sure I have you to thank."

"Not really. There was no real evidence against you. Anderson couldn't hold you for more than forty-eight hours."

"No proof? What about the video showing what I did?"

"Are you trying to get thrown back in jail?" she asked with a sly smile.

"No. Trust me, that place was disgusting." She acted as if dark entities were commonplace, and that the cops understood what they were capable of. "I'm just glad things worked out the way they did."

"Me too. Are you here to pick out that engagement ring?" Greer asked.

Too bad he couldn't tell if she wanted him to say yes or no. "Actually, I came to see you."

While she kept her expression shuttered, at least she didn't tell him to go to hell. "About what?"

This wasn't going to be easy. "Greer, not only do I need to apologize for everything I did, I'm still trying to wrap my head around what really happened and why. You seem to have a good idea about these things. Do you think we could do an early dinner and discuss them? I still have a lot of questions."

Her brows furrowed as she reached out and cupped his hand. "Are you having nightmares? I might be able to help with that."

He was pleased with her concern, but her interest seemed born out of a desire to help rather than a willingness to go out on a date. That was okay. He just wanted to be with her. Needing to think clearer, he slipped his hand out of her grasp. "Not nightmares exactly. It's more like I'm living in a fog. I thought if I understood who this man—or rather this being—was, I might find some closure."

"I see. Sure. We can meet. Will your girlfriend be there so she can understand what you're going through? It is always nice to have someone to talk to."

Fuck. He didn't want to start off with a lie. "No. I'll explain it to her later."

Just then a customer walked in, and Blake's sixth sense kicked in. Over the years, he'd developed the ability to tell the good from the bad, and this person reeked of evil. When he glanced over, Blake exhaled.

His judgment must be off, like everything else since the attack. This customer appeared to be just an ordinary guy, dressed in a nice brown tweed suit, wearing a large brimmed chocolate brown hat. The gray aura pulsing around him must be in Blake's imagination. Being around Greer probably disrupted his special abilities.

"I'm looking for something with sardonyx," the newcomer said. "Do you have anything with that gemstone?"

The blonde was waiting on the man. "Just these earrings."

"What time would you like to meet?" Greer asked, interrupting his study of the newcomer.

Blake shifted his attention back to her. It wasn't a good sign that he was so easily distracted, but he'd been looking at the energy trail coming off the man. "Is five okay? I can pick you up here."

She smiled, and his body lit up once more. "Perfect. See you then."

Not wanting Greer to change her mind, he headed off, taking

one more glance at the man who seemed so intent on buying his jewelry. As Blake exited the store, an image of Crystal popped up in his mind's eye, and he focused hard to banish it. Blake needed to concentrate. Tonight had to be about this Mange character. While this entity might be dead, Blake needed to know if there could be any more of his kind around.

You're deluding yourself. You don't give a flip about the entity. You just want to spend time with Greer, his dragon said. *And I thank you for that.*

Maybe, but remember you were the one who urged me to be with Crystal. I thought you wanted us to be together. Fickle animal.

All dragons like sex. I never said you should be together forever.

No, he hadn't, which was all the more reason why he had to find out if Greer felt the same way about him as he did about her.

"WOOWEE!" TORY EXCLAIMED as soon as Blake and the other customer left the store. "He's into you, Greer."

"You don't know that. You heard him. The poor man is confused, that's all."

Her cousin laughed. "Confused about Mange maybe, but not about you. Didn't you see how his eyes glazed teal? Or how his scales pulsed?"

His eyes did have specks of teal in them, but no way Tory could have seen any of Blake's scales—pulsing ones or not. His arms were covered, though Greer thought she saw something dark flash around his collar. Even if his scales had lit up, it didn't prove they were mates. "What about his future fiancée?" Greer challenged.

She shrugged. "He said he plans to get his head on straight and then talk with her. Hopefully, it will be to tell her the two of them can't be together because of you."

"Coming to grips with what happened doesn't imply he plans to break up with her," Greer countered. Though she wished it did.

Tory shook her head. "I think he's having second thoughts. I mean if you two really are mates, he's got to be going through hell right now wondering what to do about her. Does he let her down gently, or does he try to figure out if you're feeling the same draw before he does?"

She didn't like the idea of anyone suffering because of her, but she couldn't do much about it. "I, for one, won't judge him no matter what he decides. Tonight, I will hopefully get some answers about his intentions."

Greer was happy she hadn't committed herself to someone before finding Blake. That would have been tough having to say goodbye to the person she cared for. The real question was whether Fate had paired them. Her dragon was definitely saying yes, but her animal might have said that solely based on the fact Blake was disarmingly handsome.

I've never led you astray before. Her animal actually sounded hurt.

I agree you've never told me a man was my mate before.

See?

Greer was thankful Blake had made the first move and asked her out. It might not be a real date, but she would learn more about him.

As the time grew closer to five, Greer's nerves increased. She was always the cool one, and yet this evening could determine her path for the rest of her life. If Blake turned out to be the one... Stop it! She didn't need to be getting ahead of herself. Blake had asked her out to discuss the incident. That was all.

Or was it?

"I need to call Angelique," Greer told Tory.

"Why?"

"Blake wants to know more about Mange. I can't explain about dark and light entities without talking about her. I don't want to out her without her permission."

"You could just say an anonymous friend told you about Mange."

Greer smiled. "That'll work. If I didn't believe Blake was my mate, I'd tell him almost nothing, but he deserves to know."

Tory clapped. "I am so happy for you."

"Don't start cheering just yet. Remember, he's involved with another woman."

BLAKE STEPPED OUT of the jewelry store and headed in the direction of the bank, his concern for Crystal growing. She probably had gone back to work after dropping him home. Blake had showered as he said he would, and had even rested for a few minutes, but the need to see Greer prevented him from sleeping.

While he could go into work to see if anything needed his attention because of his unfortunate absence, he feared Crystal would see the guilt swimming in his eyes. In his frame of mind, he wasn't ready to tell her about finding his potential mate. Besides, he hadn't spoken with his boss yet to see if he still had a job. Since Blake had been taken against his will and then unjustly incarcerated, there shouldn't be any issues with him returning.

Tomorrow was Saturday, which was Crystal's day off. He'd see her that night. On Monday, he'd go in to work and pretend as if nothing had happened. No doubt he'd be bombarded with a bazillion questions about his close call with death and the subsequent arrest. After tonight's date—or rather meeting with Greer—he hoped he'd learn enough to answer all of their concerns.

The best thing for him now was to head home and try to grab a nap since he wanted to be at his best tonight. The last thing he needed was to be so tired that he blurted out he and Greer were mates. Tonight was all about learning who Mange had been. If Greer tossed him some favorable signals, he'd wing it and hint at having feelings for her.

Once in his condo, he grabbed a snack and then stretched out on the sofa with the television softly playing some tunes, ready to fall asleep. Unfortunately, his mind wouldn't stop spinning. After an hour he gave up.

A few minutes before five, Blake headed to the jewelry store. He hadn't changed his clothes on purpose, since he didn't want her to think this was a real date. In fact, he decided to take her to the Hillside café—a casual place where they mostly served sandwiches. The shop closed at seven, which implied this was a fact-finding mission only.

Even though the café was within walking distance of SinCas jewelers, he wanted to drive his Landspur—a rather high-end car. Was he trying to impress Greer? Hell, yeah. She was practically nobility and probably didn't slum it—ever.

He parked in front of the jewelry store, slid out of the car, and straightened his shirt. He shouldn't be nervous, but for some reason he was. When he rang the bell and was buzzed in, his body exploded with need. Whoa. No doubt every black scale was flashing. His teeth sure had sharpened, and his talons were trying to poke their way out of his fingertips.

Blake wasn't sure if he should be upset or excited about his body's continued reaction to Greer when he was close to her. One thing he did know was that he could no longer deny his destiny.

The worst part was that he'd have to tell Crystal about Greer, and her negative reaction would tear out his heart.

His challenge now was to figure out how to convince Greer they belonged together. That might sound like a silly concern since Greer's animal would be clawing at her too for them to be together, but if she still harbored any ill will toward him, she might deny the truth.

Greer looked up after locking the glass display case. "Hey, give me a sec. I'm almost ready."

He had to hand it to her. She was a cool one. Greer twisted her head to the side so he couldn't see if her eyes had turned purple. The change would indicate she was excited to see him. Since the lights were so bright in the store, it prevented him from seeing if her scales were flashing. Damn. His scales were so dark no one could miss them.

"No rush," he answered.

He studied the jewelry in the case, pretending to be interested, but it was impossible to focus on the intricate design of the earrings when Greer was near. Heat was rushing through his veins too fast to truly appreciate the beauty of any of the pieces.

Greer locked the case. "Let me get my purse, and we can go."

Either the blonde had already left, or she was in the back. After Greer returned, they exited through the front door. Using some kind of electronic device, she locked and alarmed the store.

"I drove since I didn't think you'd want to walk the six blocks in heels."

She laughed, and his dragon roared. "I live in high heels. Short of running a marathon, these shoes won't stop me from going anywhere."

Goddess, but he loved her attitude. "Driving is faster. Besides, the Hillside Café closes at seven."

"Then driving it is."

He opened her car door and had to avert his gaze the moment he caught sight of those endlessly long legs. How Blake was going to last through dinner without his horny dragon showing signs of his desire was anyone's guess.

He said nothing during the short drive to the restaurant, mostly because he didn't want to delve into what had happened with Mange only to stop the discussion two minutes later.

There weren't any spaces in front, so he parked in the rear lot. In silence, they entered through the back. The restaurant was only half full, which meant there were several options for seating. Blake chose one as far from anyone as possible. Scaring someone with some dark entity discussion wouldn't be good.

Greer slid into the booth, and he sat across from her.

"Tell me what about the incident troubles you the most," she said, getting right to the point.

So much for her thinking this might be a date. It didn't matter.

He really did have a ton of questions. "Why did this entity target me? Did this being have a type—young male perhaps?" Being a dragon shifter he didn't look one hundred and two years old.

"As far as we could tell, it only inhabited men. I'm guessing it picked you because you were a convenient target. This entity wanted to use me as leverage to get to my friend, and you were at the right place and the right time."

"You mean Angelique?" Her eyes widened. "That thing you called Mange mentioned her name."

"I forgot that it did. Yes, Angelique is my friend, but she is also mated to my cousin, Thane. Mange seemed to think he could get to her through me."

"I know Mange said something about her being a white entity, but what exactly is that? I know of white and dark lighters. Is she like one of them?"

Greer leaned back against the seat and blew out a breath. Just then the waitress stopped by.

"Can I get you two something to drink?" she asked.

"Coffee for me," he said.

"I'll have iced tea—unsweetened, please."

"Be right back."

Blake looked around to make sure no one was listening. "You were telling me about Angelique."

"Oh, yes. She's not a white lighter. Angelique is far more powerful than that." Greer proceeded to tell him some unbelievable story about another realm in which entities existed without bodies. These pure energy entities could be either light or dark. They were relegated to remain in that realm unless Fate needed them on Tarradon for some reason. "That's where Angelique comes in. She is a light entity who Fate sent on a mission. I don't understand how it all works, but Fate gave her a body so she could fulfill her duties."

"That is too strange. What was her mission?"

"It's on a need-to-know basis."

"Ah, I get it." He was an outsider.

She sighed. "I know this is hard to understand. Even I don't know all of it. What I do know is that somehow this dark entity either escaped from its realm or was released. We figured that because Fate didn't give it a body, his presence on Tarradon wasn't sanctioned."

"So it had to enter someone else's body in order to do whatever it had planned."

"Precisely, and since we believe its plan was to harm Angelique, who is a light entity, it decided to take me to get to her," Greer said, her tone suddenly hard.

He huffed out a laugh. "This dark entity must have misjudged your friend, because Angelique and your cousin killed him."

"They did, thankfully."

This was overwhelming. Blake had never heard of this other realm until now. "I really was a means to an end then," Blake said, his voice trailing off.

She leaned back. "I believe so."

He was thankful he'd done nothing to deserve it. "Let's hope no one else escapes from that place."

She chuckled. "No kidding. My family has been around a long time, and none of us have heard of anything like it before."

With his questions more or less answered, he wanted to bring up the delicate subject of whether they could be mates. Blake was out of practice when it came to discussing matters of the heart, and he hoped he didn't mess it up.

Chapter Three

INTERESTING. BLAKE REALLY seemed to only want to talk about why that dark entity had attacked him and nothing else. Despite their discussion being smooth and easy—comfortable even—Greer wanted to steer things in a different direction—like whether he believed they were destined for each other. She hadn't planned to bring up that topic tonight, but when he was asking her questions, his eyes had swirled with different colors a few times, and his eyeteeth had elongated a bit, implying he was excited to be around her. Too bad his long sleeved blue shirt hid any flashing scales. That would have been another indication they were fated for one another.

Not only was Blake physically reacting to her, he also seemed to be hanging on her every word. Was that the kind of reaction a man who was almost engaged should have? Or did it mean he realized they were meant for each other and would no longer pursue this other woman?

Greer inhaled. "Can I ask you something?"

"Sure. Anything."

"When we were in that warehouse and I was trying to heal you, was the sensation pleasant or painful?"

His eyes turned pure teal before looking away. "I was kind of out of it if you recall, but I do remember heat and then light pouring into me."

Light was a good thing. It meant he could feel her healing powers. She waited for him to say something else—like he had been filled with lust—but he remained silent. Damn.

"I felt this charge race through my veins," she said, trying to urge him to comment. *It is the same charge I am experiencing now. Please tell me you feel the same thing.*

Blake pressed his lips together. "Now that I think about it, it was pleasant." He lowered his chin. "Fuck. Okay, it was more than pleasant, Greer, and you know it. We're dragon shifters for goddess' sake. But was what I felt real?" He leaned forward. "I'm in a relationship with another woman, so how could it have been?"

Pain took her breath away. "I realize that, but..."

"Blake?" A female with a slightly panicked voice and heels rapidly tapping on the tile floor rushed toward them.

Blake's face paled. "Crystal? What are you doing here?"

The woman's jaw hardened. "What am *I* doing here? Picking up some dinner after I finished work because you said you were too tired to let me fix you dinner. You claimed you needed to rest. I didn't realize you had a date!" Bitterness laced her voice.

"Crystal honey, it's not what you think. This is Greer, the woman I kidnapped—without my knowledge, I might add. I needed some questions answered about what really happened and why."

So, this was his girlfriend. She was human and lovely—shoulder length dark brown hair, just the right amount of makeup to enhance her delicate features, and a dress that fit her body perfectly. Greer could see why Blake was attracted to her.

Crystal looked over at Greer. "I'm sorry that happened to you." While she sounded sincere, her voice came out tight.

"Blake needed answers, that's all." Or was it? "I was just explaining to your boyfriend here about this other realm that most people are unaware of."

Her chin trembled. "You mean Earth?"

"Not quite. This realm has entities that are made up from only light beings. The being that attacked Blake was one of the bad ones. Blake wanted to understand in order to find closure."

Crystal glanced back at him. "Why didn't you tell me you were seeing her? You didn't have to lie." Her voice softened considerably.

Blake pushed back his chair and stood. "I'm sorry. I didn't know that Greer would be willing to even talk to me after what I did."

The cashier at the counter called Crystal's name. "I have to go. I'll see you later. Maybe." The last word seemed to be an afterthought.

That didn't sound good for Blake. He must not have thought so either because he lowered his head, and his shoulders stiffened. Sympathy swamped Greer. "Go talk with her and straighten things out."

"If only I could. Hell, I barely understand what's happening myself."

I'm your mate, she wanted to say, but now wasn't the time for that conversation. "Go. I'll walk back."

"Are you sure?"

"Positive."

"You are the best."

Greer would never pressure anyone into doing something he didn't want to. After spending an hour with Blake, she knew they belonged together. The question was whether he would figure it out before he committed to Crystal.

SHIT, SHIT, SHIT. Could the timing have been any worse? "Crystal, wait up!" Blake called to her retreating back.

Because he'd asked Greer to meet him for dinner, he quickly paid their tab. He totally understood why Crystal would be upset seeing him with Greer, but he'd explained a few times about shifters and their mates. The problem was that he and Greer were interrupted just as she was about to tell him something. From the way her eyes had turned that beautiful purple, she was going to say they were mates—or was that wishful thinking on his part? If Crystal hadn't interrupted them, he might have told her himself.

Even if that wasn't what Greer was about to say, the moment he was aware of her, the spark between him and Crystal had evaporated.

Hurting the woman he'd been with for six months was the last thing he wanted to do, but Fate wasn't giving him a choice. Did he care for Crystal? Sure. He had only been with her because his mate hadn't come along yet, and he figured they were so good together that they might as well get married. Was that a great reason to commit to someone for life? Probably not.

He raced up behind Crystal and gently clasped her shoulder. "Can you stop for a minute, please?" he asked.

She spun around. "I know what you're going to say."

"What is that?"

"That she means nothing to you, but I saw the way you looked at her."

His mouth turned dry. How long had she been standing close by? "What way?"

"With lust."

That was true, but this wasn't the place to tell her. "I barely know the woman."

Damn. He shouldn't lie, but discussing this on a public sidewalk wasn't the best place for it.

"You went through a major ordeal together. That kind of things bonds two people together," she said. This time her tone held some compassion.

"It's not that way." It was more than that.

"Look, Blake. I know you've been through a lot, and I think you need to take a few days off to figure out what you want to do."

"I don't need time. Can we just talk? My car is parked in back. We can go back to your place if you want."

She exhaled deeply. "Fine, but no more lies, okay?"

"I promise."

They walked around to the lot in back where he caught sight of Greer heading in the direction of the jewelry store. Damn. He hoped he hadn't messed things up between them. He opened the door for Crystal and waited for her to be seated before closing it.

His mind raced about how to tell her the truth. Blake hopped in the front seat, started the engine, and took off. Neither said anything during the short ride back to her place. Thankfully, Crystal rented an apartment close by so she could walk to work.

Once they entered her apartment, she flicked on the lights. "Wine?" she asked.

He wouldn't have been more stunned if Crystal had pulled a gun and shot him. Not that a bullet would have killed him but still. "Yes, thank you."

Blake followed her into the small kitchen and grabbed a bottle of wine from the rack on the counter. He opened it while she retrieved the glasses.

"Is she your mate?" Crystal asked, her voice a bit strained.

"Yes." Blake had promised not to lie.

"You said there was always the possibility that you'd find her, but I didn't think it would be so soon." Her voice came out close to a whisper.

Blake's chest constricted as he poured the wine. "Let's sit down. To be honest, I truly believed I'd never be given a mate."

Crystal walked into the living room and he followed. "I'm glad you found her," Crystal said. He might have believed her if her hands hadn't been holding the wine glass as if it was a lifeline.

"You're just saying that to be nice, right?"

She sat on the sofa and patted the seat next to her. Blake joined her. "I'm not sure what I'm feeling right now. What I do know is that we are great together."

"We are, so how can you be happy that I've found my mate?" She wasn't making any sense.

"Hear me out. I've known all along that this day might come. You did warn me. It's why I've held myself back these last six months."

"Held yourself back?" This discussion was blindsiding him.

"I care a lot for you, but to be honest, I'm not *in* love with you. I couldn't let myself fall totally for you." She placed her free hand on his knee. "I've been on my own since I was seventeen, and you know how hard that was for me. When you came along—a man who was so in control—I guess I believed that you were the family I needed."

Don't let her story get to you again, his dragon said. *Greer and you are mates.*

"I can see that happening, but why were you so upset at the café just now?"

"I think I was more shocked than anything. You turned me down for a date, and I felt betrayed."

"I am sorry. I should have told you."

"It's okay." She squeezed his leg. "I had the sense you wanted to make our relationship official, but this is for the best."

His head spun. If she didn't want to be with him any longer, he wasn't going to try to convince her. He just wished she'd told him sooner. In his heart, he knew that being comfortable with each other wasn't a good reason to marry. "Where do we go from here?"

"I don't know, but I'll probably move to Hearndon Province to be near my cousins. I'm sure I can get a job there, assuming I can get my boss to write me a good recommendation." A hint of smile crossed her face. She was hurt, but Crystal was trying to make the best of it.

His head spun. "You are an amazing person, Crystal."

She stroked his face. "Thank you, but do me a favor?"

"Anything."

"Be happy."

GREER HAD A rather restless night. She couldn't help but worry that Crystal would convince Blake to never see her again. While she was convinced his dragon wanted them to be together, Blake seemed to be an honorable man and wouldn't want to hurt Crystal. As much as she admired his devotion, she hoped he understood that Fate wasn't to be messed with.

Tory came out of the back room. "Hey, good morning. How

was your date last night?"

"It wasn't a date."

"Uh huh."

"Okay. It might have been a date if his girlfriend hadn't shown up."

Tory's eyes widened. "What? Did Blake freak?"

"Kind of. She accused him of lying, because he told her he planned to stay home last night. Instead he was out with me."

"Ouch. What did he do?"

"He left with her."

Tory opened the case and rearranged some of their silver bracelets. "I'm sorry that happened, but I can understand. They were almost engaged, right?"

That had been Greer's reaction. "Yes. In his defense, Crystal was understandably upset, and I told him to go after her to smooth things out. We had already finished talking about Mange when she showed up." Greer leaned against the counter. "I will admit I was disappointed. I was in the process of learning if he thought we were mates. I mean, his eyes were flashing teal, and I swear I saw his teeth sharpen. His shirt was open at the neck and some black scales flashed. He told me that when I touched him while trying to heal him, he felt a connection."

Tory's eyes sparkled. "That means he thinks you're mates."

"Possibly, but we didn't get that far in the discussion before Crystal showed up."

Tory relocked the jewelry case. "When are you going to see him again?"

"I have no idea."

"If you are mates, I'm pretty sure he'll want to talk with you first before he does anything like buy a ring. He'll be dying to know if you feel the same. Because you are so cool under pressure, it is going to make it harder for him to know if you like him."

Heat raced to her face. "My scales were flashing, but I don't think he noticed since they are so light colored."

"Personally, I'd give him a couple of days to figure things out. Then if he doesn't reach out, you could call and ask if he has more questions about Mange. Keep it friendly."

"That is a good idea, but I don't have his number."

"I bet Anderson does. He would have asked when he booked him."

Greer smiled. "You are a sly one. I'll do that as soon as I figure out what I want to say."

Chapter Four

G REER'S PHONE RANG a few days later. When she noted it was an unidentified caller, she debated not answering it, until she realized she hadn't heard from Blake since the fiasco the other night. It could be him. On the other hand, it might be Crystal calling to tell her to bug off.

"Hello?"

"Greer," said a deep sexy voice that had her scales flashing. "This is Blake."

As if she couldn't have guessed from the way her body had reacted. "Hey. Not that I'm complaining, but how did you get my number?"

"I bribed your cousin Anderson for it."

She chuckled. "I doubt that. The man can't be bribed."

"Okay, I asked nicely."

"I'll have to thank him. How did it go with Crystal the other night?" She might as well address the dragon in the room.

"Good, real good."

Her stomach tumbled. If they had patched things up, had he called just to see if she was okay? "I'm glad."

"Do you think I could take you on a real date tonight?"

Greer almost fell over. "What about Crystal?"

"She's okay. It's partially why I wanted to see you. I also need to apologize about that night. I don't normally skip out like that on someone."

Good to know. "No, I get it. She thought there was something between us. Jealousy is painful." She should know. Stabs of it were coursing through her body right now.

"How about seven?"

It took a moment to realize he'd given her a time. "Sure. Where would you like to pick me up?"

"Your place?" He had such hope in his voice that she couldn't disappoint him. She always had her dates meet her at the store, saying she needed to work late. That way when she returned from the date, it was easier for him to drop her off there—unless she really wanted to go back to his place.

"Sure." She gave him the address. "I'll let the guardhouse know you're coming."

"Fantastic. See you then." He disconnected.

"Who was that?" Tory asked as she stepped out of the back room.

"Blake. He asked me out." The joy in her voice was evident.

Her eyes shone. "That's fantastic, but what about his girlfriend?"

"He said she was okay with things and that he wanted to talk to me about it tonight over dinner."

She grinned. "Sounds promising. Maybe he told her you two were mates, and she was cool with it."

Tory was a romantic. "I don't believe that for a minute. No woman would willingly give up Blake Masters."

She shrugged. "You never know. I can't wait to hear how it turns out."

"He's picking me up at seven at my place."

Her brows rose. "At your place, huh? This is serious."

"He's my mate."

"Then go home now and get ready."

"We don't close for another half hour," Greer said.

Tory waved a hand. "I can handle it. Half the time we're here alone anyway."

They only worked together three days a week. The rest of the time, they manned the shop by themselves. "I appreciate that."

Tory hugged her. "Good luck!"

"I don't need luck; I need to keep calm."

Her cousin laughed. "Go."

Greer took the elevator to the roof where she shifted and flew the short distance to the large field behind her townhouse. It was one reason why she chose to live on the outskirts of town—more landing room.

Even though she had more than two hours to prepare for her date, she wanted to find the perfect dress and have time to put on makeup.

Once Greer showered and washed her hair, she tried on many outfits, but she was unable to decide the best look. She should have asked Blake where they were going. That would have helped her decide. In the end, she figured what she wore didn't really matter if they were attracted to each other.

Greer ended up mixing a pair of casual dark jeans with a rather dressy low-cut green top. She let her strawberry blonde hair hang loose, and then gave her eyes a smoky look. As usual, her lip and blush colors were subtle.

The overall look was sophisticated but approachable. Perfect. Why she was nervous she didn't know. From the confidence in his tone, Blake had already decided his path, which hopefully involved the two of them.

When the doorbell rang at seven, she nearly jumped.

Settle down, she chastised her dragon.

I can't. It might be a night to remember.

No. We need to take this slow.

Who says?

The bell rang again. Sheesh. Greer hurried to the door, looked through the peephole to make sure it was Blake, and then inhaled. With a smile on her face, she opened up. As much as she had thought about this moment, nothing could have prepared her for the sight of hunky Blake Masters. He too had gone with the classy but casual look—medium colored blue jeans, black boots, and a white button-down shirt open at the throat that was topped with a navy-blue jacket. His still wet, dark hair was slicked back.

"Hey, come in."

Because she rarely entertained, she hadn't received much feed-back on her design style—other than from her family members who never understood why she'd bought a townhouse on the edge of town instead of a downtown condo.

He glanced around. "Nice digs."

"Thanks."

His gaze returned to her, her décor apparently not holding much interest to him. "You look…amazing. I see we thought alike."

She laughed, but it came out a bit strained, which wasn't her style. "We did. Let me grab my purse." She picked it up from the sofa. "I'm ready."

Once she locked up, he placed a hand on her lower back and escorted her out the front door. He wouldn't have done that if something hadn't changed between him and Crystal, right?

Once they were in his car, he looked over at her. "I should have asked what you like to eat."

"I eat anything."

"Have you been to The Fishery? It opened a month ago, and I hear it's good."

"No, but I love fish."

He smiled, and her dragon scratched and clawed. After a short drive into town, Blake snagged a parking spot in front and then escorted her inside. Jitters of excitement sliced through her. Greer had never had such a physical reaction to anyone before. If Blake didn't come out and say they were mates, she might have to be the aggressor. While capable of doing so, she would prefer he make the first move.

The inside of the restaurant was quaint yet fairly upscale. The walls were decorated with photos of lighthouses and boats, and on each table sat a candle and a vase with what looked like fresh flowers. All of the tables were covered in white cloths, and the soft lighting added to the romance.

"Good call," she said.

Blake smiled. "I'll have to thank my friend for recommending it."

The hostess seated them, and when the waiter rushed over to take their drink orders, Blake asked if she wanted to share a bottle of their house wine.

This was a date! "That would be perfect, thank you."

Blake was being so polite that she wanted to push back her chair, walk around the table, and kiss him, partly to see what her dragon would do. But Greer wouldn't. At least not yet. If she didn't do something soon though, her animal might create a stir.

"I guess I should tell you about my talk with Crystal," Blake began.

Greer couldn't tell whether she'd like it or be disappointed by the news. "From the way she stalked off, she was a bit upset."

"She was at first, but by the time we arrived back at her place, she had calmed down. After all that was said and done, I think she was relieved that she walked in on us."

That wasn't what she thought he'd say. "I'm confused. Why would she be?"

"From the moment we met, I told her I was a dragon shifter and that I was destined to find my mate. Crystal understood she wasn't the one."

Then why had he planned on buying an engagement ring? "She dated you anyway?"

He laughed. "You don't have to sound so surprised. I'm a hundred and two years old, and during that time, you and I hadn't even met. I had told her I doubted that I would ever meet my mate."

Joy infused every cell in her body. "Let me make sure I understand. You're saying we're mates?"

He stilled. "I hope I didn't get my signals wrong. I thought you could tell."

Greer actually laughed. "Oh, thank goddess. Yes, I can! I thought that since you were with Crystal that you wouldn't want to lose that affection and go with Fate's suggestion."

Blake reached across the table. "As soon as I met you, I knew we belonged together. I realize now that while I loved being with Crystal, I wasn't in love with her. There's a difference. She's not really in love with me either. We share the same interests and get along really well. I guess I thought that was all I could expect." He released her hand and then fiddled with his napkin. "Crystal is a lot smarter than I am. She knew to keep her emotions in check. Was she jealous when she saw us together? Sure, but only until I told her we were mates."

This was a dream come true. "Crystal is really letting you go without a fight?" That was hard to believe.

"Apparently."

The waiter returned with their bottle and poured them each a glass. Blake held up his, and she tapped hers against it. "To us," she said.

"To us."

The first sip was crisp and wonderfully dry, just the way she liked it. "Do you think Crystal was being honest?"

"My ego would like to say no, but my heart tells me she was. She plans to move to Hearndon Province since she has some relatives there. I told her she didn't have to leave, but she wanted to."

"She seems like a great lady."

"She is."

Greer couldn't believe her luck. Because of the joy that was skittering around her body, she was almost too excited to eat, but she would for Blake's sake. This was a date, and she didn't want to ruin it.

Once they looked over the menu, Greer chose the fish of the day, lightly fried, and topped with capers, while Blake picked the river trout in a creamy lemon sauce.

"Tell me what you do at the store, Greer."

To the outside world, her job was merely working as a clerk in a jewelry store, but as a Guardian, she was often called upon to help her family behind the scenes to carry out their mission of aiding others. For now, she'd keep that part of her life a secret.

"As you know, I sell jewelry, but it's also my job as well as my cousin Tory's to keep up the inventory. We'll order some pieces and design others. We have a lab on site where the jewelry is made. This lab also can reset jewels, as well as adjust and fix broken items. Both Tory and I do the books, as well as man the store."

"Impressive. That sounds rewarding."

"It is, actually. When a man or woman buys a piece of well-made jewelry, it brings them joy, which in turn brings us a lot of pleasure. What about you? Is working in a bank rewarding?"

He hemmed and hawed before answering. "I do like my job, but it is stressful, especially when someone can't pay his mortgage on time. I don't do the actual repossessing, but I order it to happen."

More proof he was a nice man. She sipped her wine. "If you had the qualifications for any job in the world, what would it be? A doctor? A lawyer? What?"

He laughed. "You wouldn't believe me."

This was fun. "Tell me. No, let me guess."

He tossed back the rest of his drink and poured himself another glass. "Be my guest."

"A fireman. Or maybe a paramedic." Greer didn't know why she picked those occupations, but they seemed like professions where he could help others. Kind of like the Guardians.

"You're close. I'd like to be a policeman. A detective if you will."

That surprised her. "Why? Because you like to help people?"

"Yes, and I think I'd be good at it."

She liked his confidence. "And why is that?"

"Because I have this very unusual talent of being able to sense and even see a person's essence if you will. I believe I'd make a good bounty hunter."

"You can see a person's essence? Intriguing." None of the Guardians had that ability. "Tell me more."

He leaned forward and kept his voice low. "Everyone emits a

type of electric signature that I can see and follow if need be."

"I'm not really following," she said. "My siblings and cousins each have unique talents, but none can sense someone that way. What is it that you see exactly?"

"It's hard to put into words, but it's almost like the person leaves an electronic trail behind them. I'm not saying I'm a blood hound, but as long as I can remember which essence belongs to which person, I can follow them."

"Does an essence trail have a color or a smell?"

"A color made from light. From what I've been able to figure out, the darker the gray a trail is, the more nefarious the person is. Not only can I see this kind of electric glow around them, when they leave an area, I can follow the trail. Mind you, it dissipates quickly, so it's not like I could go into a crime scene a few hours after some murder and find the killer."

Wow. He'd make a great Guardian. "That is amazing."

Now all she had to do was make sure they mated, so he could become one!

Chapter Five

B LAKE HAD NEVER told anyone about his abilities before, fearing others would consider him a freak. Nor had he heard of anyone else having a sixth sense like his. He'd told Greer because not only was she his mate, she too had magical talents—like healing. She would understand.

Greer placed her napkin on her lap. "If you want to become a detective, why don't you take some classes in your spare time? I'm sure my cousin Anderson would love to have you on the Force."

"I'm too greedy. I like my pay at the bank. But as my satisfaction decreases, I am more and more tempted to hang up that job."

He held his breath, wondering how Greer would react to having a man by her side who didn't make the big bucks.

"I think you should do whatever makes you happy. To hell with the finances."

Easy for her to say. Her family was loaded. Okay, so was his, but it wasn't as if his family handed him any of their fortune. "I might test the waters. We'll see."

"There's enough stress in life already. Do what you love."

He couldn't agree more, but his definition of happiness would be making love with Greer. If he played his cards right, it might even happen tonight. While he'd promised himself he wouldn't rush things, his body hadn't received the memo.

They spent the rest of the date talking about growing up in Edendale, except that he left out a few important details—topics that weren't first date material. Throughout their talk, he was surprised they had never run into each other, especially since her family did business at his bank. Maybe if his father had been in the mining business, it would have been different.

By the time they had finished the bottle of wine and eaten their meal, they had chatted about everything other than their future together. By then, the restaurant was emptying out. It was time to leave. Blake decided to let Greer take the lead whether or not to ask him back to her place. She was a classy woman who seemed to have her own way of doing things. Too bad his dragon had been scraping and shooting fire in his gut all night long.

After Blake paid the bill, they left and had just seated themselves in his car when inspiration struck. For the last two years, he'd been with a human. While he had no problem flying around with Crystal in his grasp, she'd never been comfortable with that kind of transportation. With Greer, they could both fly side by side, and that realization exhilarated him.

The question was where would she like to go at night that was romantic? Checking out the stars was the first thing that came to mind, but that sounded a bit clichéd. Or was it? "I have an idea," he announced.

It was a little dangerous to show her this spot, but that was the chance he had to take. Disliking secrets, he'd have to tell her sooner rather than later anyway.

"What's that?" she asked.

"It's only ten. What do you think about flying somewhere? To be honest, I don't want our time together to end."

Considering how dark it was in the car, he couldn't be positive if her eyes had turned purple or not, but her arms sure were flashing up a storm. It looked like heat lightening gone wild. Yes!

"Sounds awesome. Where do you have in mind?"

"How about if I surprise you?" Hopefully in a good way.

"I love it. Let's park at my place, and we can take off from there."

"Perfect."

After he parked at her townhouse, the two of them walked

around to the back. The night was clear and crisp, perfect for what he had in mind. "Just follow me," he said. "It's maybe a ten-minute flight."

"I can't wait."

Blake shifted, and when Greer did too, his dragon shot out fire.

Stop it! he chastised.

Her colors are glorious, his dragon said.

They are indeed. Her black shiny scales interspersed with light yellow ones made her a shimmering goddess. He hoped she liked that he was mostly sand colored with black scales placed at random intervals.

Not wanting her to think he'd turned to stone, Blake shot upward. A second later Greer was by his side.

GREER HAD FLOWN next to her siblings and cousins numerous times during a battle, but that experience was nothing compared to what Blake and she were sharing right now. Just being with a man like Blake did something to her soul. It also might be that she wasn't used to seeing such a gloriously colored dragon. The black scales were just the right touch to his perfect look.

The clear skies and gentle breezes lifted her spirits. At first, she thought he'd take her to the mountains where they could watch the stars, but he was headed away from the tall hills. For once, she'd go with the flow and just enjoy being with him.

About twelve minutes later, he dipped his head and soared downward. Greer followed but was rather perplexed. The only thing below them was a huge estate belonging to Dr. Hanson Wilshire, the highly sought-after cosmetic surgeon. No one in her family had ever used his services, but many who entered their jewelry store had.

The castle interior was mostly dark, but a few lights glowed, implying someone was home. To her surprise, Blake landed on top of the main turret. As soon as his feet hit the cement, he shifted, and she followed suit.

"What are we doing here?" she whispered. "I doubt the owners will be happy that we're trespassing."

He laughed. "My parents are on vacation, and my two sisters don't live here anymore. Only a very small staff is present. I'll let them know I'm here so they won't worry."

Greer was speechless. His parents owned this place? How was that possible? The last names didn't match. He walked over to what looked like a computer screen next to the door, pressed a button, and announced he was on the roof. He then asked for someone to bring up a bottle of wine and two glasses.

Blake spun around. "All set. Have a seat."

Greer turned around. She hadn't even noticed there were lounge chairs there. "I'm confused. Your last name is Masters. I thought this place belonged to Dr. Wilshire."

"He's my stepdad. My dad split when I was three, and Mom remarried two years later. Hanson is like my father. I even call him Dad."

"That's wonderful." She wanted to know everything about him and his family.

"I didn't mention it before because I didn't want you to think differently about me. While I make a very good living as bank manager, it's nothing compared to what my father has. His money is his though, not mine."

She smiled as she slid down onto the padded lounge chair. "I get it. The Caspian family owns a ton of land and makes a lot of money in the mining business, but it's not like they give it to us kids."

"We're more alike than I realized."

A knock sounded and then a door that must have come from a stairwell opened. A man wearing a shirt with a logo on it stepped out, carrying a tray.

"Master Blake. Your wine."

"Thank you, Craig. Just put it down. I appreciate you coming up so fast."

"Of course, sir. Will there be anything else?"

Blake looked over at her. "Do you need anything?"

"No, thank you."

"Very well, sir." With that, the man disappeared as silently and as quickly as he had arrived.

Greer leaned her head back and studied the inky black sky. Other than the yellow light above the door leading into the castle stairwell, the area was quite dark. While she could see both her wine glass and Blake because of her shifter eyesight, the stars were easy to identify against the black backdrop. "This is incredible."

He sipped his wine. "I used to come up here as a kid all the time and let my imagination run wild."

She smiled. "What did you dream about?"

He chuckled. "That I was the captain of my own spaceship, flying to some planet where I would save those oppressed by tyranny."

"You wanted to be a hero even then."

"I suppose."

"Why go into banking? It doesn't seem to be your passion," she said.

"I have my stepdad to thank for that. He was a huge proponent of education. I excelled at numbers, and my attention to detail was, if I don't mind saying so myself, quite remarkable, so the job of managing money seemed like a good fit. I came from a good family who taught me not to take money or education for granted." He paused for a moment. "I do have one vice."

"Which is?"

"I love fast cars."

She laughed. "There are worse things you could spend your money on."

Blake shifted to his side to face her. "I suppose so. What about you? What do you like to spend your money on?"

"I'm rather shallow. I've always had an affinity for clothes and makeup." She held up a hand. "Not that I don't have a more serious side. I help support The Spiegel House Orphanage. I know how lucky I am to have such a wonderfully supportive family too, and I want to help those who are less fortunate."

Blake reached out and squeezed her hand, and that one touch lit her up. He was similarly affected since his black scales shown against his sand colored ones. He let go. "If we light up anymore, we might not be able to see the stars."

His exaggerated statement made her laugh. "You are funny."

"I like you, Greer. Really like you."

"I like you too."

Greer relaxed. They'd finally admitted—albeit it subtly—that their relationship could go to the next level. Wanting to enjoy the moment, she sipped her wine and studied the sky.

"Amazing, isn't it?" Blake asked.

She wasn't sure if he was talking about the stars, the wonderfully rich, full-bodied wine, or the fact they'd more or less claimed they wanted to be together. "Absolutely."

For the next few minutes, they sat mostly in silence, occasionally commenting on a constellation. Most of the time Blake was the one who knew the star cluster's name, proving he had spent a lot of time in these chairs.

The longer they sat, the more comfortable she became. At the same time, her body was heating up from the inside, making it more difficult to sit still. Her dragon seemed to be pacing inside of her, if that was even possible.

Blake reached out and clasped her hand. "Thank you for coming with me," he said.

"Really? Did you think I wouldn't?"

"I don't know you all that well, but I'd certainly like to."

She liked that sentiment. "Then how about coming back to my place?"

Greer was never this forward, but Blake clearly was letting her decide when to indulge in their desires.

"I thought you'd never ask." He popped off his seat and held out a hand. "My lady."

She laughed once more. He was being so silly. After he let the staff know they were leaving, they shifted and took off. The trip back to her townhouse seemed a lot shorter, but at the same time it took an eternity. Since she'd decided she wanted to get down and dirty with this man, her townhouse couldn't appear soon enough.

When she spotted the location, she soared to the ground and landed behind her home. Blake was beside her seconds later. Both shifted. Not wanting to spoil the mood by talking, she merely threaded her arm through his and led him into her townhouse through the back door.

Once inside, she flipped on the hall light, but before she could even spin around, Blake had her pressed against the door.

"I've wanted to kiss you for so long. I can't wait any longer," he said.

"Then don't."

Chapter Six

BEING AGGRESSIVE WITH Greer had not been Blake's goal, but he couldn't help himself. Sitting on top of the turret in his special spot brought back memories of yearning for a mate. Now that he'd found this incredible woman, he didn't want to waste another moment. He'd expected to be consumed with guilt over Crystal, but her admission that she'd never loved him had washed away his worry.

Greer slipped her hands under the lapels of his jacket and slid his coat off his shoulders, letting it drop to the floor. As much as he wanted to impale her in the entryway, that was no way to treat her. Their first lovemaking experience deserved something better.

"I want you so much, but maybe we should take this elsewhere," he said. "I don't want you to think I'm an animal."

Greer looked up and smiled. "That's one thing I like about you. You are an animal. But I agree, the bed would be much more comfortable."

Facing him, she walked backward while she lifted off her top. His pulse skyrocketed at the vision of her skimpy black lace bra and those mouth-watering tits. Holy goddess of Fate. His cock turned so hard he was convinced it would burst through the zipper. For sure his eyes were flashing teal, and his scales were pulsing so hard it was almost painful.

She tossed her shirt on the back of the sofa and smiled. He wasn't sure if he could make it up the stairs before he succumbed to his overwhelming lust. "You are so beautiful."

Blake had wanted to be a little more poetic in his description, but his brain wasn't functioning at full capacity at the moment.

"If you take off your shirt, I'm sure I will be just as impressed," she said.

She didn't have to ask him twice. After undoing the cuffs and then fumbling with the first few buttons, he decided to hell with it and lifted his shirt over his head. Now past the sofa, he just tossed it on the banister leading upstairs.

Even though she didn't look where she was going, she knew when to lift her foot onto the step. Wanting to have his skin against her as quickly as possible, he unsnapped the top button of his jeans.

"Uh, uh. That's my job." Greer wagged a finger at him as she kicked off her high heels and left them on the stairs.

After toeing off his shoes, he deposited them next to hers.

Not able to stand this teasing any longer, Blake took two long strides toward her, swept her off her feet, and rushed upstairs with her in his arms.

At the top of the landing, he stopped. "Which way?"

"Second door on the right." Her wide grin made his heart trip.

Blake carried her to her bedroom and toed open the door. She reached behind him and flipped on the light. He'd expected everything to be neat and perfect—like Greer. Instead, about five discarded tops and two pairs of slacks sat on top of the neatly made bed. He set her down, not sure if she'd want to make love on her clothes or not.

"Give me a sec." Greer gathered her things. With her arms full, she placed them on top of the dresser and then spun around. "Where was I?"

Her gaze zeroed in on his chest and then dropped to his crotch. Under her hot perusal, his dick throbbed. "I think I was about to help you out of your jeans," he said. If he didn't get her naked soon, his dragon might try to make an unwanted appearance.

"Not yet, you don't. My house. My rules. And I have a plan for you."

"Bring it on." He wasn't about to argue with her. Greer's aggressiveness excited him. He might sound brave, but it was highly possible he would crumble under her touch.

Eyes flashing purple and her skin glowing, Greer looked like she was on a mission. "Your pants have to go," she said as she approached him.

As she unzipped his jeans, Blake unhooked and then unzipped hers. Her brows rose. "Hey, all's fair and all that," he said.

She laughed as they both tugged at the same time. Her jeans slid effortlessly off her body. His? Not even close. The material caught on his jutting erection.

"I see we have a problem," she said.

"We do. What are you going to do about it?"

More of her scales flashed. "This."

As if time stood still, Greer lifted his briefs and pants over his cock and lowered them. Just as he was about to step out of them, Greer dropped to her knees, grabbed his dick, and drew it deep into her mouth.

His balls pulsed and his scales glowed. The skin on his back began to harden—a sure sign his dragon was ready to escape.

Stand down, he chastised his animal. If his stupid beast turned his arms into claws at the wrong moment, he might hurt Greer.

I can't help it, his dragon shot back. *I've never experienced anything like this before.*

Before Blake could continue his conversation, Greer cupped his balls and squeezed gently. His mind went blank.

To keep from exploding, he grabbed a handful of her hair and wrapped it around his palm. When she reached around him and grabbed his ass, he lost it. His climax shot out so powerfully, it embarrassed him.

He pulled back, and Greer let go. "I'm sorry," he said.

The last thing he expected was for her to smile. "It was my goal to make you lose control."

"Why?"

"It will take away all my guilt when I come multiple times."

He chuckled. "You are something else, Greer Caspian. Let's see just how many times I can make you do just that."

GREER HAD NEVER been that bold in her life. It was as if she had been possessed—and not by some dark entity. Being with Blake—her mate—had changed her.

He grabbed his briefs and cleaned himself up. "It's my turn to excite you."

"I'd like that."

He lifted her up and placed her on the comforter. In one quick flick, Blake had her out of her bra. His eyes flashed, as did his scales. "You are amazing."

Not that she didn't love hearing how much he enjoyed her body, there was a time for talking and a time for doing. Greer drew him toward her, and then cupped the back of his head. Blake's response was to slide his knees between her legs. When she dragged him closer, his eyeteeth sharpened. And so did hers. The kiss was not so much sensual as it was one born out of desperation and need. Their moans came out loud and with increasing frequency as their tongues battled for dominance. Greer dragged her palms up his back, loving how his muscles bunched with every move.

Blake broke the kiss. "I don't have any protection with me. I'm sorry."

"Don't worry. I've already taken precautions."

He smiled. "Good to know. Now where was I?"

"Returning the favor?"

He huffed out a breath. "I totally forgot. I must have been carried away with the kiss. Being with you seems to shatter my ability to think."

"No problem. I loved that kiss and will be demanding more in a moment."

"What did I do to deserve you?"

She dragged a finger across his lips. "You were in the right place at the right time." Blake might not see it that way, but she did.

Blake winked and then slid down so that his lips were on top of one of her nipples. "Mmm."

He drew the tip into his mouth and sucked hard, sending ripples of delight across her body. Arching her back for more pressure, she dug her now sharp nails into his shoulders. Just as he switched to the other side, his cell rang.

He didn't stop, but she could sense the tension in his movements. The sound wasn't just a ring. It was more of an alarm. "Maybe you should answer that." Those words had been really hard to say. In reality, she wished it would just stop.

"Fuck. It's the bank. That alarm means there's been a breach— or a power surge." He crawled off her. Once he retrieved his jeans, he stuck his hand in the pocket and lifted the cell.

"Masters here." He paced, asking only a few questions before disconnecting.

"How bad is it?" she asked, though from the look of disgust on his face, Blake was troubled.

"I have to go. I am so sorry."

Greer sat up. "What happened?"

"I'm not sure. The bank alarm went off, but no one seems to know the cause. The cops are on their way, but they need me to see what was stolen."

"That's terrible. Call me, okay? Or return when you are done?" she asked.

"I'd really like to, but it's already almost midnight. By the time I speak with the cops and check things out, you'll be asleep." He slipped on his jeans, wadded up his briefs and stuffed them in his pocket. The rest of his clothes were downstairs.

Greer jumped off the bed and snagged a robe from the closet before trailing after him.

After he finished dressing, he clasped her shoulders. "I want to make this up to you."

"The break-in—or whatever it was—wasn't your fault. Stuff

happens." She'd lost track of the times the Guardians had needed her help, and she'd been forced to leave a pleasant situation.

"How about I pick you up tomorrow at five, and we go on a picnic in the park to watch the sunset? Afterward, we can continue where we left off."

Blake was such a dear man. "I'd love that."

He stepped closer and kissed her. "Dream about me."

She smiled. "There is no question about that."

Possibly so he wouldn't change his mind about leaving her and rushing to the rescue of the bank, Blake hurried out.

Those kisses had been so amazing that Greer had wanted a lot more, but she'd have to wait until tomorrow when she and Blake went on that picnic before she was able to enjoy more of them. Having a mate who was romantic was a dream come true. He was everything she'd ever wanted. Not only was he a dragon shifter, he was smart, came from a good family, and was hotter than hot.

The only thing they lacked was good timing. How messed up was it that Blake had received an emergency call just when they were in the middle of making love? The answer? It was extremely messed up.

Considering how her body was still vibrating with need, Greer retrieved a wine glass from the cabinet and poured herself a drink. She'd stay up for another hour in the off-chance Blake's emergency had been nothing.

With her glass in hand, Greer moved to the sofa and sat in front of the television. She turned it on, hoping to find something interesting to watch. Close to one, her cell rang. It was Blake.

"Hey," she said.

"I hope I didn't wake you."

"No. I was watching some television waiting for your call."

"You didn't have to do that."

"I wanted to. How did it go?"

"The cops were all over the place when I arrived, but nothing seems to have been taken, at least not that I've been able to tell."

"That's odd, considering the alarm went off."

"I know, right? If I didn't know better, I'd say Fate was trying to keep us apart."

"Don't be silly. She's the one who brought us together, remember?"

"I know."

"Are you coming back here?" she asked.

He sighed. "I wish I could, but they're still investigating. It will be a really late night. You need to get to bed. I'll meet you in front of SinCas Jewelers tomorrow at five. I'd say earlier, but I know what I'll be doing for much of the day tomorrow."

She didn't want to guilt him in to coming over now. "I'm sorry you have to do this, but tomorrow sounds wonderful. Don't stay up too late. We have unfinished business to attend to."

"You don't have to remind me."

When he disconnected, Greer pressed the phone to her chest and sighed. She had it bad. Real bad.

Chapter Seven

B LAKE SHOULDN'T LET the agitation of waiting get to him, but he'd been so close to finally making love with Greer that his dragon was still acting up. Had his phone not sounded an intruder alarm, he would have ignored it.

"I think we figured out what the issue was," the police officer said, tapping his tablet.

"What was the problem?"

"It looks like an animal chewed through the alarm's wiring, which set it off."

That sounded lame to him, which meant he would be here at the bank to double-check that someone hadn't taken something or hacked their systems and downloaded any account information. "Thanks, officer. I'll see about having the wires replaced."

"Good idea."

By the time the cops cleared out, it was close to three in the morning, and Blake was tired. His apartment was thankfully above the bank. Living there meant he had no commute in the morning. It also meant that if anyone tried to break into the bank, he could be there in a flash—unless he was at Greer's house.

Speaking of her townhouse, while it was nice, his building had a great rooftop terrace, which made taking off and landing convenient. Also, his apartment was larger than her place, but he didn't want to get ahead of himself, even though having her move in with him would be fantastic. Besides, her jewelry store was a mere three blocks away.

The false alarm call was making their separation worse. It didn't matter he could still smell her scent on his hands and body. When he closed his eyes, he could visualize her writhing under him, loving his every touch and kiss. Shit. His cock was pressing so hard against his zipper, the discomfort jarred him out of his daydreaming. *Focus*. It was time to go.

As soon as he locked up the back, he headed up the stairs to his condo. After showering and then downing a beer, he dropped into bed. Too bad his mind refused to shut off. Greer's breasts and lips kept floating in his mind's eye. Between his rock-hard erection that refused to go down and a dragon that kept up a dialogue about how much he needed Greer, Blake's sleep was sporadic at best.

Once he realized that real sleep was not going to come, he crawled out of bed. He tossed back a strong cup of coffee and then headed down to the bank to double-check that he hadn't overlooked something last night.

Even though the cops had checked everything, Blake wanted to be thorough. He went through the surveillance tapes again, as well as checked their computer system several times, but nothing appeared to have been tampered with. By the time he was convinced the alarm had been caused by a hungry gnawing animal, it was close to four in the afternoon. Time to clean up and head to the grocery store to pick up food for their picnic.

After shopping and placing the prepared food in his backpack, he left to meet the woman who had haunted his dreams. His plan was to casually comment that the Helpful Healing Shop was open today and then suggest they stop in. Blake wanted to pick up something for her to make up for ducking out on the most amazing time of his life last night.

The shop was normally closed on Sunday, but his cousin Nan managed the store. It took a bit of persuading, but she agreed to open up just for them. Blake had no idea if Greer ever shopped there, but the items Nan sold seemed like the things Greer would like— being a healer and all.

Blake wouldn't have thought of the idea, except he remembered seeing not only yellow salt lamps there, but red ones as well, and red was the color of the high heels Greer often wore. According to Nan, the red salt lamps gave off the strongest aura. Its stated purpose was to relax a person, and right now they both could use some relaxation. It seemed like a scam to him, but his cousin swore by it. Besides, Blake wanted to show Greer that he was sensitive to her needs.

When he pulled up in front of her jewelry store, she was standing there wearing shorts, sandals, and a low-cut pink top that would make it really hard to get through their picnic without insisting he take her back to her place and finish their lovemaking session.

Just as he was about to slide out and open the car door for her, Greer pulled it open and hopped in. "Hey."

Her smile lit up her face and made his scales glow. "Sleep well?" he asked.

"Let's just say a certain man kept entering my dreams and waking me up."

He laughed. "I had the same problem."

Greer sobered. "Did you ever figure out what caused the alarm to go off at the bank last night?"

"Our best bet was an animal chewed through some wires." He explained how he'd spent most of the wee hours of the morning and then all day at the bank checking things out.

"I'm sorry."

"I'd rather have it be an animal than some hacker."

"Good point."

He edged into the street and headed toward the park. Four blocks from his destination was his cousin's shop. He pulled to the curb and cut the engine.

"Why are we stopping?" she asked.

"I wanted to buy you a present." Pretending as if he just happened to notice the store was open sounded lame.

"I didn't do anything."

He smiled. "You most certainly did. You didn't make a fuss when I had to run out on our amazing date."

"I understand emergencies."

"All the more reason to give you a present." He held up a hand. "If you don't believe you deserve my gratitude, then consider this a random gift, given from my heart for my mate."

She grinned. "I certainly can't argue with that, now can I?"

"No." Blake was thrilled that Greer understood. He jumped out of his car. This time, Greer waited for him to open her car door. When she saw the name on the store, her eyes widened. "I wouldn't have thought you would step foot in a store like this."

Blake never wanted to lie to her. "My cousin runs it."

"Really? Then by all means let's see what she has to offer."

Nan grinned when he walked inside. "Glad you could make it."

"Nan, this is Greer Caspian. Greer, this is my cousin Nan." They shook hands. He faced Greer. "I kind of picked out something for you already," he said.

"That is so sweet. I'm sure I'll love it since everything in here is my style." She turned to Nan. "How long have you been open?"

"Just a couple of months."

Blake was thrilled he'd chosen wisely. He led her over to the lamp section and picked up one he'd found. "I really liked this one."

Greer ran a hand over the stone. "It's sardonyx."

"I didn't know what kind of stone it was, but I liked that it was red because it matches the shoes you often wear."

She hugged him. "You're sentimental. I had no idea."

Greer wandered around the store for a bit and then picked up some jars of cream, which she insisted on purchasing. Blake paid for his gift, and Nan placed in a nice bag. "I hope to see you again," Nan said.

Greer smiled. "You can count on it."

He hadn't told Nan about Greer being his mate. For some reason, he wanted to keep it a secret a little longer in case something went wrong.

As they left the store, he carried both bags while she threaded her arm through his. Blake couldn't be happier. The park was only a half-mile away, but he wanted to drive in case he needed to take Greer back to her place in a hurry. He didn't trust his dragon not to exhibit signs of neediness, so Blake parked close to the spot he'd chosen to have their picnic.

From the back, he retrieved a blanket. "How about you carry this, and I'll grab the backpack with the food?"

"I can do that."

After a short walk, they found a spot overlooking the lake. He bet it would be wonderfully romantic to watch the sun set from there.

GREER WAS BLOWN away by how amazing Blake was. Sure, he felt bad about leaving her last night, but if someone had broken into the bank, Blake had to check it out. She could see the tables being turned at a future date, especially if someone was injured, and she was called upon to heal that person.

"Help me spread out the blanket," Blake said.

"You weren't kidding when you said we'd have a real picnic."

He smiled. "Never." Once the blanket was in the right spot, he set down the backpack and opened it up. "We have fried chicken, two kinds of salad, bread, and wine."

This was such a guy picnic, but she loved it. "How about you open the wine, while I set out the food?" she asked.

"Can do."

In companionable silence, they prepared their picnic. Her stomach grumbled at the amazing looking spread. Sitting shoulder-to-shoulder facing the small lake, they grabbed what they wanted.

At the first bite of chicken, Greer's mouth watered. "Good call on the food."

"To be honest, I was a little nervous since I wasn't sure what you liked to eat."

She placed a hand on his arm. "I told you I eat just about anything. And you? What kind of eater are you?"

"Not picky at all, though I do love fish."

While Greer wanted to talk about how incredible the start of their lovemaking had been, if she turned her thoughts in that direction, her dragon would want instant satisfaction. Sitting on a blanket in the middle of a park wasn't the best place to make out. She'd heard many times how important the Caspian image was.

They were halfway through their meal when a car alarm sounded less than a block away.

Blake pulled his phone from his pocket. "Fuck. It's my car. Excuse me."

Blake was up and on the run before she could put down her food. Greer hoped someone had just bumped into his car and set off the alarm. Worst case, someone had targeted him for some reason. That, or else she had a *secret admirer* she was totally unaware of—someone who didn't want her to be with Blake.

One of the buildings blocked the view of his car, preventing her from seeing what was happening. The annoying noise stopped, and two minutes later, Blake returned.

"Well?" she asked.

He shook his head. "All the doors are still locked, so maybe someone just bumped into my vehicle."

"Anything's possible."

"Unless I go to the trouble of having the cops check for finger-prints on the door handles, I'll never know." Blake smiled. "Right now though, I have more important things to concern myself with—you."

She leaned over and kissed him. Big mistake. Her scales flashed, and her body heated up. If she thought she was the only one who was excited, she'd be wrong. The more time she spent with Blake, the harder it was to keep her hands to herself. Using all of her restraint, she pulled away. "That was nice, but we can't start something," she said.

"I agree. I promised you a picnic and a sunset. We'll wait until the sun goes down and then we'll head back."

"Sounds good. The view here is wonderful."

Blake kept his gaze on her. "I like this view better."

She laughed. "Behave." That was easy to say but hard to do.

They finished their meal, mostly talking about the stresses of Blake's job in between bites. "Don't get me wrong, there are times when I love to be able to help either a business succeed or a family acquire their dream home, but when I have to turn down a loan, it doesn't sit right with me," Blake said.

"I think all jobs come with ups and downs. You just have to focus on the happy side of what you do."

"I like the way you think," he said.

She smiled. "On that note, how about we clean up and take our discussion someplace more secluded?"

As much as Greer wanted to sit and admire the afterglow of the pinks and oranges of the sinking sun, her body was demanding something else.

"You are a woman after my own heart."

Blake stuffed the uneaten food into his backpack and then helped her fold the blanket. He dumped the trash in a nearby can as they walked back to his car. He opened her door, and then went around to his side and climbed in. Blake shoved the key into the ignition, started the engine, and pulled onto the road. The only thing Greer could think about was stripping him naked and finally making love to him.

Ten minutes later, Blake pulled in front of her townhouse and parked. From the back she gathered her wonderful present and new creams. While she loved all kinds of scents and mood lighting, she'd never taken the time to decorate her place to incorporate her love of healing.

Inside, she set the gift on the table in the corner of the living room and placed her purchases on the kitchen counter. "I think the lamp is perfect there."

Blake plugged it in, and then said nothing for a few seconds. "I don't feel any calmer."

"I don't think it works that fast. Besides, I have a feeling our dragons are keeping us from being calm."

He turned toward her. "You got that right."

"How about joining me upstairs?" she asked.

"I'm right behind you."

Chapter Eight

BLAKE WAS BURNING up inside. It had taken all of his willpower to casually eat dinner and watch the sunset. On the drive back to her place, all he could think of was making Greer his—not mating with her yet—just making love to forge the bond between them.

Halfway up the stairs that led to her bedroom, she took off her shirt and let it drop on the treads. The manner in which she disrobed implied she was as desperate as he was.

Once in her room, Blake clasped her arm and gently spun her around. "Come here, sexy lady."

Greer palmed a hand on his chest, looked up at him, and tossed him the most alluring look. "What are you going to do?"

"This."

Blake leaned over, pulled her hard against his chest, and kissed her.

Mate, mate, his dragon chanted.

I know, but we need to do this right. I only get one mate, once in a lifetime.

Then hurry.

Blake wanted to hurry, but he also wanted to take his time to savor her and pleasure her the way she deserved. He inhaled her delicious scent, enjoying having her in his arms. When their lips firmly pressed together, his need exploded. No one had ever tasted sweeter. With their tongues tangling, and his fingers threaded through her hair, Blake was transported to what could only be described as some kind of heaven.

Then as if an unknown force entered the room, it pushed them toward the bed. Somehow they ended up sprawled on top of the spread. The moment his body was fully pressed against hers, his cock demanded freedom.

Blake rolled off her.

"Why did you stop?" Greer asked, acting bereft.

"If I don't take off my clothes, and then yours, my dragon will show himself."

"I think you'll be needing some help then."

He wasn't sure if that meant she'd finish taking off her clothes or help him with his, but either way, the sooner they were naked, the better it would be. As he removed his shoes and pants, Greer finished undressing. This time she didn't leave on her undies.

"I liked the red," he said.

"I'll model them for you afterward."

The last item to ditch was his T-shirt. Once naked, all he could think about was enjoying her—and lasting as long as possible. He arranged her on the bed and then crawled on top. Decisions, decisions. Breasts, lips, or pussy?

Her breasts beckoned.

The first suck had his dick harder than metal, but that only made his dragon more desperate. Greer was sweet and perfect. With one hand, he cupped her breast, loving how she filled his palm. With the other, he first dragged his knuckles up her cheek and then drove his fingers into her luxuriously long strawberry blonde hair.

Greer groaned and heat poured into him.

Don't do anything stupid, he told his dragon.

It's hard. I want her.

So do I.

Trying to ignore his need to sink his cock into her, Blake slid lower until his cheek was against her delicious mound. He swore he could hear her pussy calling to him, so he dipped two fingers into her opening and pressed on the side, eliciting a loud groan. Yes! He loved a receptive woman.

Her rather sharp nails dug into his upper back and caused the black scales under his skin to flash on and off in a random pattern. With each pant, his scales fired in fast succession.

Desperate to taste her, he withdrew his fingers and flicked his tongue across her opening. The skin on his back hardened. Focusing only on her, he forced his body to calm down, but it didn't work.

"I need you," Greer begged, as her scales flashed faster and faster too.

"Soon."

Blake wanted to bring her to climax several times before he impaled her. He needed Greer to experience the same thing he was feeling—the excitement, the thrill, and the overwhelming lust.

He clutched the inside of her thighs and widened her legs as he continued to taste and tease her. While what he was doing might ratchet up her desires, it was also driving him crazy. Greer clutched the spread and lifted her hips. Her mewling cries, followed by a low moan and a big shudder, signified she'd come, just as he'd hoped. As much as he wanted to lick her into another frenzied state, he feared one of their dragons might emerge.

It was time to satisfy both of their beasts. Not able to hold off any longer, Blake slid up her body. The moment his dick found her entrance, he drove in. Heat seared his insides, and his dragon rejoiced.

Never before had his scales flashed so hard or his teeth sharpen to such points. Not wanting to cut her with his nails, he fisted his hands and kissed her. Stroke after stroke, he found nirvana inside this amazing woman. Their tongues went from seductively slow to desperately fast.

Greer threaded her hands under his arms only to scrape her nails down his spine. From the way her eyes were rolling back in her head and her hips were pumping, she was being transported someplace wonderful too.

"Blake, I'm close," she murmured.

He didn't need any encouragement. With one final push, his cock sent his hot seed into her. The pulsing and throbbing continued, as he remained entombed inside her.

A moment later, her body went limp, and Blake had to work hard to control his breathing. Wow. This was where he belonged. Not wanting to put too much weight on her though, he rolled them over, bathed in the wonder of it all.

Greer lifted her head from his chest. "I'll get something to clean us up."

He flipped them over again. "Better let me get something."

Blake ducked into the adjoining bath, grabbed a washcloth, and wet it. He'd just cleaned her up and himself when a click sounded downstairs. He might not have thought much of it had Greer not bolted upright.

"Someone's here," she whispered.

Shit. "Stay here," he commanded.

He dragged on his pants and raced downstairs, taking two steps at a time. If it was an intruder, he couldn't chance him getting near Greer. She might claim to be some powerful dragon who could fight, but he wasn't going to take the chance that she wasn't more than just a healer.

The front door slammed shut. Shit. Inside a house, Blake could take down most anyone. But outside, in his dragon form, he was unstoppable. As much as Blake wanted to catch the thief, he didn't want to leave Greer alone.

An engine sounded and then tires squealed. The intruder was getting away. Blake looked out the window and caught sight of the car and the first two digits of the license plate. Damn. At least the man left an electric aura trail, one that would forever be forged in his brain. It was familiar. The dark gray tinge was similar to the one coming off the man who'd visited Greer's store. Whoever he was, Blake would find him, of that he had no doubt.

Despite Blake's excellent night vision, having the lights on inside the living room would help him see what damage this person had caused. Blake flipped them on, but nothing looked disturbed. Good. He must have scared off this person before he had the chance to do anything.

As he was about to head back upstairs to check on Greer, he noticed the present he'd bought for Greer was missing from the table. Now that pissed him off. The bag that contained his gift was on its side where before it had been upright, but her creams were still on the counter.

The bedroom door opened and then shut. Crap. He didn't need Greer trying to play the hero. She raced downstairs. Thankfully, she had put on clothes. "What happened?" she asked.

"Someone stole your present. I'm going after him."

"Oh, no." Apparently, that present meant a lot to her. "Wait for me. I'm going with you."

"Greer, he's getting away. Stay here, please?"

She crossed her arms. "Fine."

"I won't be long, I promise."

Blake dashed outside and shifted into his dragon form. The lingering gray trail from the intruder indicated that he'd dashed from the front of her house to his car. Tracking him while in his vehicle would be more difficult but not impossible.

GREER GAVE BLAKE a minute head start before going after him. Once outside, she shifted into her dragon form and then cloaked herself. Being a Guardian sure came in handy sometimes. It wasn't that she thought Blake couldn't handle some petty thief, but part of her wanted to see him do his tracking thing.

The decision to cloak was because she didn't want him to become distracted if he realized she was nearby. Even though she understood they would be mating in the near future, she wasn't ready to spill the fact that she, her siblings, and cousins were Guardians.

Greer followed Blake even though she had no idea why he was headed toward the woodlands. Nothing was out there. As far as she could tell, only three or four cars were traveling in that direction. If one was being driven by the thief, how could Blake tell which person had broken into her house?

Quite a while later, when the cars disappeared under the dense foliage of the forest canopy, Blake did a large arc and turned around. His ability to track must have been hindered by the trees. Darn.

Not wanting any kind of lies between them, she uncloaked herself and flew in his direction. Only then did it occur to her that he would have known she'd followed him because he would have seen her essence trail once he turned around. She doubted even cloaking could disguise that.

She wasn't able to tell if he was surprised to see her or not, but she imagined the conversation would be a fairly heated one once they returned to her place.

After they landed in her backyard, they shifted at the same time. "Learn anything?" Greer asked, trying to act as if it was totally normal that they'd been chasing after the thief.

"Just that he was lucky there were other cars nearby or else I would have landed and ripped him out of his driver's seat."

Okay. She hadn't expected the fairly mild-mannered Blake Masters to be such a badass. She opened the back door to her townhouse. "I could use a glass of wine. You?"

He came in behind her. "Why did you follow me when I asked you to stay put?"

Thankfully, he didn't sound angry. "I wanted to see you in action. I was cloaked, so the intruder wouldn't know I was there."

A slight smile lifted his lips. "Uh huh. Who are you kidding? You would have interfered if you thought I needed help."

Damn. She couldn't keep anything from him. At least he hadn't asked her how she was able to cloak herself. As far as she knew, only the Guardians were capable of that feat. "Maybe."

"We'll discuss this at a later date. We need to call the police."

She spun around. Greer was used to having her family of Guardians take care of things. "Are you thinking he left some prints or something?"

"Maybe. Regardless, someone stole something, and we should report it."

When he pulled out his phone, she placed a hand on his arm. "Let me call my cousin Anderson."

"I thought he was a homicide detective."

"He is, but I'm family. I bet he'll oversee the theft."

"Go for it," Blake said.

She called Anderson on his personal cell. "Greer. Is everything okay?" he asked, his voice almost shaking.

"I'm okay, but someone broke into my house." She explained what was taken. "I think we interrupted him."

"We?"

"Blake and I."

Her cousin cleared his throat. "I'll be right over."

"Thank you!"

She faced Blake. "He'll be here as soon as he can."

"Good. Back to the topic of why you followed me downstairs when I asked you to stay put."

She didn't need to be dealing with this right now. "I can take care of myself."

"That may be true, but what if he came back and totally ransacked your house while you were flying with me?"

"Things can be replaced. Besides, if he had come, don't you think it was better that I wasn't home?"

"You might be right, but tell me this. If I had managed to stop this guy's car and he had an accomplice, what would you have done?"

"I would have fought him right along side you." Greer lifted her chin.

"In hand-to-hand combat?" he asked.

Yes, she could do quite well in that department, but now wasn't the time to explain how. "I would shift into my dragon form. Look, I also went after you because I wanted to make sure you were safe."

She moved closer and ran a hand down his chest.

His eyes widened. "You wanted to take care of me? I assure you I can do that myself."

This was getting them nowhere. "I'm glad to hear it. Now, how about that wine?"

He chuckled. "You are one stubborn lady. Yes, I'd like a glass."

Good. Blake's anger seemed to have dissipated. She'd poured them each a glass. Half way through her drink, a knock sounded on her door. From the familiar dragon signature, it was her cousin. Greer opened up to find Anderson and two other policemen at the door.

"Thanks for coming so fast."

Anderson nodded at Blake and then shot her a questioning look. Clearly, he was confused why Blake was there. She decided it would be best to tell the truth. Greer motioned Anderson off to the side. "I know it seems odd, but Blake and I are mates."

He let out a breath. "I see. I appreciate you telling me."

"And I appreciate you not judging."

He smiled. "Never where you are concerned. Do you want to tell me what happened here?"

Between the two of them, she and Blake told all three officers what they knew.

Anderson turned to Blake. "You said you followed the thief as far as the Woodland entrance to the forest?"

"Yes."

"How could you tell which car was his?" Anderson asked.

"I saw the getaway vehicle. It was a dark blue Camron, but I was only able to see the first two letters on the license plate number, and they were, LM."

Anderson took notes. "That's good information, though I wouldn't be surprised if the car was stolen."

"If he ditches it, we're back to square one."

"I'm afraid so, which is why we'll dust for prints inside the house and on the front door handle," Anderson said.

"The salt lamp he stole was on the table over there," Greer said.

"We'll be thorough. We don't know if he searched before he took the lamp or just grabbed the first thing he spotted. Have a seat," Anderson said. "This may take a while."

Good thing Greer had a well-stocked wine cabinet. It was going to be a long night.

Chapter Nine

"WHY IS THERE a closed sign on the door?" Greer asked Tory as she stepped inside the shop the next morning.

"Dad called a meeting."

Her pulse soared. "Is it about the theft at my house last night?"

"What? Your place was broken into?" Tory asked, grabbing Greer's arm. "Were you injured?"

"No. I never saw him." Greer held up her hands. "We scared him off before he took much."

"Whoa, whoa, whoa. We?"

So much had happened in the last couple of days that Greer wasn't sure where to begin.

She inhaled deeply. "As you know, Blake and I went out to dinner, and let's say it became obvious to both of us very quickly that we are mates."

Tory grinned and then clapped. "I am so happy for you."

"Me too. Long story short, we went back to my house and ended up in my bedroom. But, before we progressed very far, Blake received a call saying something had happened at the bank."

"Don't tell me he had to leave?"

"Yes, but it wasn't to talk to Crystal or anything. Turns out that some animal had chewed on wires that led to the alarm, but he still had to spend hours trying to figure out if they'd been hacked or if anything had been stolen. To make it up to me, he suggested we go on a picnic yesterday."

"Ooh, that sounds romantic."

"It was. What's more, his cousin owns The Helpful Healing

store near the park that sells crystals, herbs, potions, you name it."

"I know the place."

"I've never been in it before, but I picked up some nice face creams. I will definitely return when I have more time to look around. Normally, she's closed on Sundays, but she opened up just for us."

Tory sagged. "That is so sweet."

"I know, right? Anyway, Blake ended up buying me this sardonyx salt lamp."

"I've always wanted one of those."

"So have I. Anyway, we went to the park to watch the sunset and to have a picnic. Everything was perfect. Afterward, we went back to my place. We were upstairs doing you know what when we heard a noise downstairs."

Tory clasped a hand over her mouth. "Don't tell me that Blake rushed downstairs to look what caused the noise?"

Greer chuckled. "Yes. By the time I dressed and made it down there, the intruder had run off. I hadn't even realized he'd stolen my lamp until Blake told me."

"Oh, no. That was a present from Blake."

"I know."

"Did the thief take anything else?"

"No. Blake might have scared him off before he could grab anything else."

"Hmm. I wonder if this guy saw you buy it or something? How else would he have known you had it? Unless, he didn't know what he'd find when he broke in. In that case, it was random."

Her comment made her think of something. "That reminds me, Blake's car alarm went off while we were at the park, but when he went to check on it, no one had broken into it. A passerby might have seen the item in the back seat. No wait. It was in a bag, so I don't know how he would have seen what it was."

Griffin tapped on the hallway jewelry store door and then pushed it open. "Meeting is about to start," her brother said.

"We're coming," Greer and Tory said in unison.

She turned back to Tory. "Do you know what this meeting is about?"

"Dad just said that Anderson would be there."

"I doubt it's about what happened at my house. If he's here, it must be serious. The last thing we need is another dark entity roaming about killing people."

"I didn't ask for specifics, but Angelique would have warned us if there had been another breach. Come on," Tory said.

When they stepped into the large meeting room, the place was packed. The only ones who seemed to be missing were her brother Camden, her cousin Ramsey, and her father.

Uncle Jamison tapped the desk. "Everyone please take a seat."

The mumbling quieted even though a few were still at the coffee station filling up their mugs. Eventually everyone sat down, and the room stilled.

"I asked Anderson here because it concerns not only two members of our community but a breach in our portal security."

A lump formed in her stomach. Portal security was serious. Greer rarely was assigned portal duty, but those Guardians who manned it regularly were vigilant to keep out anyone who didn't belong in Tarradon. Apparently that someone had failed.

Anderson pushed back his chair and stood. "I'll get right to the point. Most of you—or rather all of you—know Betty Tisdale. Four days ago she was murdered."

Greer's heart fluttered. Why hadn't she learned of this before? If nothing else, her cousin should have mentioned it last night. Most likely he didn't want to add to her burden with more news of violence. The recent dark entity attack, coupled with the break-in had unsettled her.

Betty Tisdale was a human who had mated with a werewolf. She was in her mid-seventies and had been a waitress at the Hillside Café where she and Blake had their first *date*—the date where Crystal had barged in on them. All of the Guardians went to the Hillside Café and knew her very well. Betty was loved by all of them, which made her death even harder. "How did she die?" Greer asked.

"Wolf attack."

Her stomach sickened. She couldn't imagine being mauled to death. "Do you know who is responsible? Please don't say her husband. He is such a nice man."

"I don't know who is responsible. At first, I thought it might have been Henry, but only because he's a wolf shifter. It certainly wasn't because I thought he was capable of doing such a thing. Though after what that Mange character did, nothing would surprise me anymore. I spoke with a few of the neighbors, two of whom told me Henry had gone to Earth—to Silver Lake, Tennessee specifically—to visit his sick brother but had returned the morning Betty died."

It was always tricky when anyone went from Tarradon to Earth. If someone saw a person appearing out of thin air, it would raise a lot of questions. It was why the portals were usually located in out of the way places.

"Someone must have picked him up since it would have been a long hike to town—too long I suspect for Henry." She'd heard all the stories about the portals from Chelsea and Finn. "Maybe the person who transported him could tell us Henry's frame of mind when he was there."

"I don't know who met him at the portal, but it's not important, and I'll tell you why in a moment," Anderson said. "According to his next-door neighbor, when Henry returned from Earth, he seemed a bit off, but she assumed it had to do with his family issue."

"If you want, I can contact Ophelia, who can ask their detective for information about Henry's visit," Uncle Jamison offered.

Anderson held up a hand. "I already spoke with Detective Kalan Murdoch."

Finn's eyes lit up. "You spoke with Kalan? How is he?"

Anderson smiled. "He's great. In fact, he asked about you and Chelsea."

"You went to Earth?" Declan asked. "That's a rather extreme move just to follow up on a clue."

"I did. I went because I was getting nowhere with the investigation here, and I was determined to find Betty's killer. Even though a few claimed Henry had returned, he was nowhere to be found. Besides, I always enjoy a trip back there this time of year." A small smile lifted his lips. "The fall colors are amazing."

Maybe she and Blake could go next year. She bet he'd enjoy that. Greer's mind wandered for a bit. Shit. She needed to focus!

"What did you find out?" Declan asked. He'd recently been to Earth to get help for Angelique.

"I spoke with Henry's brother, who confirmed that he had left the morning of Betty's murder. When Detective Murdoch and I went to investigate the portal site where Henry was logged into, we found him. He was dead."

Chatter erupted. Greer couldn't believe both were gone. "Then why did his neighbors say they spoke with him?" she asked.

"That's why I'm here. I need answers."

"How did he die?" she asked.

"Another wolf attack."

Uncle Jamison tapped the table to quiet everyone. "I checked the portal logs of those who entered. It claimed that Henry Tisdale entered our portal as scheduled."

"I was the one on duty that afternoon," Birk said. "It was Henry all right. I'll swear to it."

That made no sense.

"Fuck." Everyone turned to Finn. "Sorry. I think I might know what could have happened. Did Kalan happen to mention if it was a red moon the day Henry died?"

Anderson's face paled. "He mumbled something about it, but I didn't ask him what it meant. Why?"

Finn blew out a breath. "We have these rabid werewolves in Silver Lake called Changelings who've been around for as long as I can remember. They possess a lot of magical abilities and have caused an endless amount of issues for everyone in town. If they are in their wolf form, they are easy to spot. Their eyes glow red." He shivered. "To me, they look like they've been possessed by the devil."

"That's a horrible thought," Greer said. "I hope they weren't possessed by some dark entity from way back when."

The room buzzed with speculation until her uncle tapped the table once more. "Let's focus. Go on, Finn."

He sat up straighter. "While we eventually managed to take down a few of their council members who were basically thieves, they are still around today. Now however, they are disorganized and probably more dangerous because they are desperate."

"Why would they want to harm someone from Tarradon?" Declan asked. "I didn't think many on Earth even knew of our realm."

Finn shook his head. "Few are aware of its existence. I'm going out on a limb here, but Henry could have been in the wrong place at the wrong time. The lifeblood, so to speak, of the Changelings is sardonyx. It's what gives them their magic. A Changeling might have somehow learned that we mine the stuff here. To us, it's not all that useful. To those on Earth, it is."

"You said sardonyx?" Greer asked.

"Yes, why?" Finn and the rest of group shifted their focus to her.

"That's what was stolen from my place last night."

More rumbling exploded. "You were robbed?" Griffin asked. Her older brother was highly protective. It was one reason why she hadn't called him last night. He'd have insisted she move to the safe house.

"Yes, but I was in bed at the time. I heard a noise." She saw no reason to mention that Blake was with her, even though Anderson knew. "By the time I threw something on and went downstairs, no one was there. A sardonyx salt lamp that I'd just gotten that afternoon was missing. I called Anderson, and he came right over."

Anderson nodded. "We dusted for prints, but so far, we've come up empty handed. The guy was careful."

Tory briefly raised her hand. "It's probably nothing, but on Friday, a man came into the jewelry store asking about anything containing sardonyx."

"I remember him," Greer said. "I didn't pay much attention because I was speaking with Blake at the time. I can ask him if he noticed anything about the man."

"Thanks." Anderson turned back to Tory. "What did this man look like?"

"He was maybe five feet eleven, fairly fit, and looked about fifty years old, but with shifters, one never knows."

Anderson scribbled down some notes and then looked up. "If there is a connection between the theft and the murders, I'm not sure what it is. My question is how the hell did he get by you, Birk? You know Henry."

"It was Henry all right. I even chatted with him for a bit." His eyes dimmed. "Now that I think about it though, all of his answers were kind of vague, almost as if he didn't know what to say. I just figured he was distracted because of his ill brother. But if Henry was dead at the time, who was that person?"

Finn lifted a hand for a moment. Her uncle nodded. "Birk believed he was talking to Henry Tisdale, because on Earth, during the red moon, if a Changeling touches someone he will take on that person's appearance."

Everyone talked at once.

"You mean like Mange?" Anderson asked, as soon as everyone quieted.

"Not exactly, but close. Mange inhabits a person. The Changelings merely look like the other person who usually has no idea there is a doppelganger out there. Furthermore, the Changeling can only hold onto the image of the person for two to three days—at least that is the case on Earth."

"I still don't see why he'd have to kill Henry, assuming the killer was a Changeling," Anderson said.

Finn shrugged. "If they were both at the portal at the same time,

Henry would know this man was impersonating him. It's possible Henry confronted him, and then the man killed him."

If that were true, that would be a real tragedy. "If these magical werewolves need sardonyx, then it's possible the man who stole the lamp from me could have been the same man who came into the store. Considering he is a werewolf, it's possible he was the one who killed both Betty and Henry," Greer said. "It's just a theory though."

"It's an excellent concept, but if someone from Earth is here to steal sardonyx, the guy is a ghost," Anderson said. "If for some reason he shows up at the store again, call us immediately."

Birk kept tapping the table. "I messed up. I'm sorry."

"You couldn't have known," Uncle Jamison said.

"I still feel responsible. I'm going downstairs now and ask Chris to pull the video feed for the store last Friday. Maybe we can get an image of the guy. If we do, I'll send everyone a copy."

"Everything is circumstantial at this point, so we can't apprehend him. He might be an innocent bystander," Anderson said.

They all mumbled their thanks. Birk pushed back his chair and strode out. Sheesh. First, it was an entity from a different realm, and now one of Earth's creatures was here. They needed a break from all this madness.

Chapter Ten

JUST AS ANDERSON was about to leave, his phone rang. He held up a finger to quiet the group. "Excuse me," he said. He returned his attention to the caller. "This is Detective Caspian." He listened for a good thirty seconds. "Is he dead? I'm glad. I'll head on over now. Thanks." He disconnected and then addressed the group. "I have no idea if these two cases are connected, but someone just attacked mine owner, Gregory Malpan."

"Shit," Declan said. "How is he? Not that I liked the guy, but I don't want to see anyone else harmed."

"He's alive," Anderson said.

"Did a wolf do it?" Greer asked.

"I don't know. I'm going over to the hospital now to get the details. Malpan's finally conscious, so hopefully, he'll be able to tell us who attacked him and why. I'd love to get an identification even if there is no connection to the man who killed Betty and Henry."

"It's probably someone he cheated," Declan mumbled under his breath.

"I'll let you all know what we find out," Anderson said, acting as if he hadn't heard Declan's comment.

"Do you think the two cases could be connected?" Uncle Jamison asked.

"Probably not, but Malpan is one of the few miners, besides yourselves, who mine sardonyx. Bottom line is everyone needs to be careful. If there is another maniac on the loose, we have to be vigilant."

A moment before Anderson reached the door, Birk rushed in.

Everyone turned his attention to him. "You find anything?" Anderson asked his cousin.

"I had Chris look at the video feed. While it shows this mystery man coming into the store, the guy kept his head down the whole time. The hat he was wearing shaded his face. It was almost as if he knew where the cameras were located."

"I don't know how he would know that. I've never seen him in the store before," Tory piped up. "And I'm good with faces."

Greer shook her head. "I've never seen him before either."

Anderson blew out a breath. "Look, we have no proof that the man wanting to buy jewelry made from sardonyx is anything other than a customer. However, I'm hoping Malpan can shed some light on it. Don't worry, we'll find who killed Betty and Henry sooner or later." Anderson pulled open the door and left.

Uncle Jamison stood. "I know Anderson is on this case, but we need to put out some feelers. Use our network and maybe warn anyone going back to Silver Lake that it could be dangerous. If one of these Changelings got through once, more might come."

As if Uncle Jamison's word was law, they shoved back their chairs and took off. While she had debated not telling Blake what happened because he'd want to search for the guy himself, she didn't want any secrets between them.

BROTHER RICHARD HAD found the mother lode of sardonyx! The only thing dampening his joy was that he'd barely escaped town with it. Good thing he was able to enter the forested area before that damned dragon shifter got a hold of him. He had to admit it had shaken him to the core. He'd been in this place less than a week, and the number of dragons flying overhead had been unnerving. While he had never seen any of these creatures attack a person, their size alone was enough to scare the crap out of him. He was thankful these beasts never had the desire to go to Silver Lake.

As soon as Brother Richard no longer sensed the dragon, he'd stashed the stolen car in a dense patch of foliage along the side of the road since he couldn't afford for the police to find it. If they did, he'd be screwed for many reasons. The last thing Brother Richard needed was to be arrested and kept in jail indefinitely for illegally entering this dragon-loving place. Moreover, he didn't relish returning to the city on foot—even in his wolf form—both of which would be tough.

Once he stepped out of the car, he undressed and then tied his prized possession in his shirt. After he shifted, he took off for his lair deep in the forest where no one would find him.

Even after traveling on the uneven path for twenty minutes, he had no problem locating the spot where he'd been staying for the week. He'd marked it well. Wanting the sardonyx safe, Brother Richard dug a deep hole and dropped his valued asset inside. While the amount of sardonyx would be enough to power his Changeling Clan for a while, he wanted to take home more. He alone would save his Clan.

The issue was that he wasn't ready or able to go back to Silver Lake yet. That would take some research on how to do it. Clearly that portal thing was the ticket, even though he'd never heard of anyone mentioning they'd used portals before. Thank goodness, he remembered the location where he'd arrived, so at some point, he'd return home the same way he came.

The return trip notwithstanding, he wanted to find more of this magical rock to secure his Clan's future.

All Richard had to do now was wait for the next red moon, touch someone about to enter the portal and take his place. That was assuming that same man wasn't standing watch, asking all sorts of questions. If that were the case, returning might be harder than Richard first thought.

Brother Richard had already tried using his phone to call one of his Clan members to let him know where he was—not that he knew his exact location—but he had no service. Maybe he'd have to steal someone's phone and give it a try. He certainly couldn't afford to buy a new one. While the man and woman he'd killed had some kind of foreign money on them, he would have to ration it if he planned to stay another few weeks.

When he'd first stepped through that ring, he thought he might end up someplace familiar, but boy had he been wrong. Only by studying the storefront windows this past week was he able to figure out he was in a town called Edendale, wherever that was.

Granted, the money here was different, but that didn't mean all that much. Most countries had currency different from the United States. Oddly enough, none of the cars were a familiar brand, but he did spot someone with an iPad. He could only conclude that he was on some remote island, which might be why there were those flying dragons circling overhead all the time. One big plus of landing here instead of someplace else was that the weather was warmer than in Silver Lake, and secondly, everyone spoke English.

His trip to the jewelry store the other day had merely been an excuse to scope out the shop for sardonyx. While they didn't have what he wanted, a bonus was finding the stunning woman with the strawberry blonde hair. Hell, he'd nearly salivated when he first noticed her. At night, he couldn't stop thinking about what it would be like to taste her. The problem was if she accepted a date with him, once they started chatting, he might let something slip about Tennessee and prove to her that he didn't belong.

THE NEXT AFTERNOON, Brother Richard returned to town. Not that he was following the stunning jewelry store woman or anything, but when he happened to spot her enter some spa store, he decided to see what she was up to. Had she not been with a tall man who looked as if he could break anyone in half, this might have been his one chance to bump into her and strike up a conversation. Shit.

When Brother Richard casually glanced in the window to check on the lady, his heart had nearly stopped from the rush. There was enough sardonyx in the store to keep the Changelings safe for a long time. Unfortunately, the store also had surveillance cameras in every corner. If at the end of his time in Edendale, he'd found no more sardonyx, for sure he would return and take whatever he needed.

Yes, it would be best if he could just purchase a few lamps instead of resorting to stealing, but he had little money. Not only didn't he have any credentials with him to get a job in this town, his skills as a landscaper might not transfer well. Too many of the plants and tree species were unknown to him. Other than the fact this place had a ton of sardonyx, it sucked.

After stealing the sardonyx lamp from the woman's house and almost getting caught, he decided it might be better to find someone who mined it instead. This morning, while he was in a coffee shop, Brother Richard had overheard two guys talking about Gregory Malpan's copper mine. When they mentioned the vein of sardonyx his workers had unearthed, his ears perked up. He figured this miner guy might be his ticket to fame. So off he went to have a little chat with Mr. Malpan. Too bad when he spoke to the owner about cutting a deal, the guy ended up being a whining, sniveling, fool who refused to deal. He had been such an asshole.

The only good thing to come out of the trip was that right before Malpan passed out from his beating, Malpan told him about the Caspian mines. According to him, they had the mother lode of sardonyx, and Brother Richard couldn't wait to take it off their hands.

THE SINCAS JEWELRY store had been open for an hour when Thane showed up with several small cameras in hand.

"What are those for?" Tory asked her brother.

"Security. We have cameras installed near the ceiling, but none are at counter height." Thane stuck one right under the lip. "This way we'll be able to see their faces and possibly catch someone who is an expert at sleight of hand."

Greer went over to check out his handiwork. "No one will be able to come in here and avoid being caught on camera."

Thane smiled. "That's the point!"

For the next half hour, her cousin installed the devices, and Greer actually felt more secure knowing that no one could steal something and get away with it. His or her face would be in cyberspace for life. When Blake had first come in and attacked her, there had been a lot of blind spots in the store. Now no more.

For the rest of the day, Greer worked hard to stay focused on her job. While she couldn't see the bank from the front of the store, she knew Blake wasn't far away, and that thought kept her libido going crazy. She had it bad, though in a way, Greer considered it a good thing. It meant they really were mates.

"Are you going to see Blake tonight?" Tory asked once their customer left.

"I haven't heard from him today, but I wouldn't be surprised if he just stopped by."

As if she were psychic, her cell rang. She snatched it out of her purse and checked the caller ID. "Well, what do you know? It's Blake."

Tory grinned. "Answer it, cousin dear."

Greer smiled. "I'll take it in the back room."

Tory laughed. "That's smart. I don't want to be any more jealous than I already am."

Greer smiled and stepped into the back room before taking the call. "Hey."

"How are you? Any more men looking for sardonyx?"

While his tone held some humor, she almost shivered. "No, and if anyone comes in, we have enough cameras positioned around to see every face. Thane installed a ton of monitors today. I wasn't watching carefully, but I believe he put some in the display case. That way, we'll be able to see everything a person is looking at."

"That's fantastic." Noise sounded in the background, but she couldn't tell if he was in an office with the door open or in a larger room. "I was wondering if you'd like to come over to my place tonight for dinner?" he asked.

"You cook?"

He laughed. "Absolutely. Just because I was raised with hired helped doesn't mean I don't know my way around the kitchen."

"I apologize for assuming. To be honest, it was because you were a man that I drew the conclusion, and that was wrong of me."

He chuckled. "No problem. It's a common misconception. Truth is, once my mom married Hanson, my parents were always going to benefit concerts or to some party. As a result, they weren't home a lot, so I hung out in the kitchen. Teresa was our head cook, and she took me under her wing. I learned a lot."

"I'm thrilled. My cooking skills are sorely lacking. What time would you like me?"

"Seven?"

"I'll be there. I know you live above the bank, but how do I get in? You said it was secure."

He gave her the passcode for the entry in back. "Just come hungry."

"Oh, I will." Hungry for him.

When she returned to the store, Tory was helping another customer. From then until closing, it turned into a revolving door of people, which was a good thing for business, but not so good for her nerves. She couldn't wait to have one peaceful night with Blake—one without interruptions.

BLAKE WAS ACTUALLY a bit nervous about this evening. He wanted to see Greer; correction: he needed to see Greer. She'd become like a drug. While that might seem crazy to an outsider, it was the truth. He'd never felt like this before with any woman.

While he did want to have dinner with her, he had a hidden agenda in asking her to his place tonight.

The outside door to his apartment opened, causing his body to heat. He glanced at the security camera, even though he knew it was Greer. Hell, he could sense her, but he wanted to see what she was wearing.

Big mistake. At the sight of her short denim skirt and cute white T-shirt, his cock turned rigid. Forcing down his strong urges, Blake pressed a button that unlocked the inside door. She stepped into the entryway and took the stairs. Oh, how he loved the sound of her heels as she climbed the steps up to his apartment. He stood at the entrance with the door open. When she rounded the bend, she looked up, saw him, and smiled.

"Welcome," he said.

"Good thing I work out. That is one long set of stairs."

He chuckled. She wasn't out of breath at all. "I've thought about installing an elevator, but I often enter from the roof."

"Cool."

Greer stepped inside, and her scent made his dragon jump. Blake's scales were flashing black against his sand colored ones, matching the speed and intensity of Greer's light-yellow ones. He leaned over and kissed her. It was the welcoming kind—not too deep. As much as he wanted to do more—a lot more—if he started, he might never stop. "Care for some wine?"

"Sure." She hesitated for a second, as if she had expected him to sweep her into his arms and press his body against hers. That would come soon enough.

"Red okay?" he asked.

"Perfect. This is really nice," she said, looking around. "I expected you to be more of a modern guy."

He chuckled. "Remember, I grew up in a castle. I was surrounded by old shit."

She laughed. "This hardly qualifies as old. Everyone seems to own leather sofas. Your cloth one is nice. I like the comfortable and clean look."

"Thank you." Blake poured the wine and handed her a glass and then held up his. "To mates!"

"To mates."

She sipped her wine and then set the glass down on the kitchen counter. Her eyes shone purple, and her arms flashed. "I wouldn't mind another hello kiss."

"Let me turn off the oven. I don't want to burn dinner."

Greer grinned. "How long do you expect to be kissing me?"

"Forever." He placed his glass on the counter next to hers and then jogged to the stove to turn it off. When he returned to her side, he scratched his chin. "Now what did I come over here for?"

"This," she said.

Greer wrapped her arms around his neck, and when she stood on her toes and kissed him, pulses of need and lust nearly felled him. He drew her close, and his body felt as if it was catching on fire from having her breasts plastered against his chest. The kiss turned into a feast. Greer ran her hands up and down his back. Somehow, in all the mental chaos, she managed to remove his shirt without breaking contact. Good thing he'd unbuttoned his cuffs, or she'd have struggled a bit.

"I think we need to take this someplace else. You up for a little air?" he asked.

She leaned back. "You want to go outside?"

"Do you trust me?"

"Of course."

That meant the world to him. "Come on and take your glass. I had planned to show you this after dinner, but I can't wait." Blake led her down a hallway that ended at a door. "This leads to the roof. The bank let me do a little remodeling."

"How nice of them."

Blake couldn't wait to show her—or rather he couldn't wait to make love to her under the stars.

Once they stepped onto the roof, Greer stopped. "Oh, my goddess. It's amazing. I love all of the lights."

The rope lights trimmed a small area in the corner where he'd put a doublewide chaise lounge. He'd stacked it with a ton of pillows and a big blanket to keep Greer warm if she got cold. Of course, he could have always warmed her up with some flames of his own.

"Don't let your parents see this," she said.

He chuckled. "Why not?"

"They'd be jealous. This is nicer than their turret."

That thrilled him. His goal had been to make this spot romantic. He planned to spend many nights up here with her talking about deep topics, studying the stars, and making love.

"Have a seat," he said.

As soon as she sat down, Blake slid next to her and lowered the back of the chaise so that it lay flat.

"Snazzy. You thought of everything, didn't you?" she said as she dragged his head down so that their lips were an inch apart.

"All I've thought about was making love with you."

She smiled. "You always say the sweetest things, but how about showing me?"

"Oh, I plan to." Now for the feast of a lifetime.

Chapter Eleven

GREER WAS ON fire. If she wasn't careful, her hands would become flamethrowers. No matter how many times she was with Blake, she couldn't seem to get enough of him. Being with her mate was seriously throwing her off balance though. Greer had spent her whole life being in control. The moment she met Blake, her life had become unhinged—mostly for the better, she might add.

When he lowered his head that last inch and kissed her, she swung a leg over his thigh and crawled on top of him. Her breasts plastered against his body, causing his hard cock to press against her stomach. Sparks flew. Their tongues tangled, sending wild waves of need through her. As wonderful as this was, she needed skin-to-skin contact.

She rolled off of him. "I'm way overdressed."

"I can do something about that."

Greer had been about to suggest they finish undressing themselves to make things move faster, but the moment he slid his hands under her shirt and lifted it up, she realized this was so much better. After he removed her blouse, he took off her bra that thankfully unhooked in the front.

The moment they finished ditching their shoes, she couldn't wait any longer. "Your turn," she said, though all that was left were his pants and briefs.

Once they were both naked, Blake pulled her on top of him, his warm skin heating her through and through. She wiggled her hips. "I do love how your body is hard in all the right places."

He laughed. "I love that you are soft in all the right places." Just as she was about to kiss him again, he rolled her onto her back and slid down until his lips found her breasts. "Especially these."

He took both of them in his hands, pressed them together, and then licked one nipple and then the other. Desire swamped her. Her nails sharpened, and her light-yellow scales gave off a bigger glow than the string lights around their little area.

Dragging her hands over his broad shoulders and down the top part of his back, her fingertips thrilled every time he flexed. Greer loved his power and his size. For the first time in her life, she actually felt petite.

As he slid lower, the cool air puckered her wet nipples, but she didn't care. He heated her up from the inside—or else it was her dragon who was shooting flames up and down her spine. When Blake swiped his tongue across her clit, she bucked.

"That feels so good," she gasped.

He looked up and smiled but didn't stop his sensual assault. Possibly because he sensed she might be cold, he lifted his arms and cupped her breasts. His dexterous fingers twirled and plucked the slightly swollen tips while his tongue did an exotic tattoo on her pussy.

Blake looked up through hooded eyes, his black scales pulsing and flashing against his lighter ones. When Greer started to pull away from him, he drew up onto his knees. She sat up, and with a slight touch to his right shoulder, Blake clearly figured out that she wanted him on his back. Once flat, he dragged her on top.

"What are you going to do, dragon lady?"

"Just you wait and see."

She straddled him. Blake snatched the blanket from beside them and dragged it over her shoulders and back. The warmth and caring made her fall in love with him even more. This was where she wanted to be. Greer leaned over, pressed her breasts against his chest, and kissed him.

The pressure started off soft but then grew stronger as their need overtook them once more. When some of his talons poked through his fingertips, he fisted his hands. The fact he was so on edge ratcheted her desire further. But it was time. Almost too excited to continue, Greer grabbed his cock, rose onto her knees halfway, and aimed. When she slid down on his hard shaft, she swore some scales formed on her back, but she mentally banished them. A groan escaped from deep inside of her. What this man did to her.

Once fully seated, she leaned over. Blake lifted up and feasted on her breasts while his fingers from one hand slid up her cheek and then threaded them through her hair. Between the clear night air mixed with his masculine scent and all of his sensual touches, her climax built too fast.

Oh, how she loved every stroke of his cock, every lick of his tongue, and every touch of his hand. Blake Masters set her on fire.

Blake grabbed her hips and moved her back just enough for his lips to reach hers. The kiss was not slow or seductive in any way. Rather it spoke of desperate need. After almost a hundred years of searching, both of them had finally found their mate.

The faster their tongues dueled, the faster she pumped her hips. Her dragon was yelling, cheering, and swooning all at the same time, hastening her brimming climax. They moaned, touched, and fucked. As if her flashing scales were blinding him, he closed his eyes, broke the kiss, and turned his head. The rope lights illuminated his sharp teeth, but she doubted he would bite her tonight. Soon she'd insist he did though.

On the next thrust, he yanked down on her hips to seal them together and came hard. Greer's climax exploded a second later, and the yell that came out didn't sound like it could have possibly come from her—yet it had. Blake grit his teeth and pressed his sharpened nails into her skin, but the slight pain only added to her pleasure.

Once her climax ebbed, Greer collapsed onto his chest and tucked her hands under his warm skin. Blake adjusted the blanket once more to make sure she was covered. He then rubbed her back. "It gets better every time," he said.

"It does at that."

After they rested, they more or less cleaned up using his briefs, and then dressed. With their wine glasses in hand, they headed downstairs to finish cooking dinner.

"I have an idea," Blake said as he tested the meal.

"I'm listening."

"Partly because that maniac who stole your lamp is still at large, and because I want to be near you, what do you think about moving in here with me?" He held up his hand. "Before you say you can take care of yourself, wouldn't you like to be down the street from where you work?"

"That is a plus." He didn't need to convince her. "I've never lived with a man, so it will be an adjustment."

"Ah, you think because I'm not as neat as you that there will be a problem? Not to worry. I can change."

She laughed. "Famous last words. It's okay. Just because I like things orderly doesn't mean your mess—assuming you make one—will bother me. I did grow up with many brothers—and trust me, they weren't given any awards for being orderly."

He lifted her hand. "I realize it's fast, but just knowing that creep can come back and break in will have me distracted all day, and I want to know you are safe at night."

Greer was a little disappointed that his reason for asking her to move in seemed to be to make sure she remained safe. That meant she'd have to do everything in her power to make him want to be with her because he was falling in love with her, like she was with him.

"Then I say yes. After we find this creep we can reevaluate."

Blake leaned over. "I'm hoping to convince you to never leave my side."

Okay. Never mind. He did want to be with her. Greer couldn't believe her luck. "After we eat, how about we go back to my place so I can pack a few bags. I'll call Thane and ask him to install more security cameras, so if this guy tries to break in again, we'll have him on video."

Now it was Blake's turn to smile. "I like the way you think."

IT WAS RIDICULOUS for Brother Richard to still be shaken up this long after the huge dragon had followed him from that woman's house, but the fear of burning to death by fire still gave him nightmares. Fortunately, today had been better. A lot better. He'd pickpocketed two people, and the poor suckers had never suspected a thing. The extra cash allowed him to have one fine dinner. Good times for sure.

Now it was time to go for a run and explore more of Edendale and the surrounding area. He doubted that it only had one portal station, and Brother Richard was determined to find them all so he could return to Silver Lake a hero.

He parked off to the side of the road where his stolen car would be hidden from view. After shifting, he took off. A bit paranoid that someone might find his buried sardonyx, he went to his *campsite*—if wolves even had campsites—and checked that it was still there. Once he was certain his hidden hole remained undisturbed, he headed out to enjoy some freedom.

Another plus about this place was that the trees were taller and fuller than he was used to, which somehow helped soothe his soul. Brother Richard couldn't be happier with the way things had turned out. Sure, he'd heard of a place where dragons roamed about freely, but he hadn't believed it. He sure did now though.

When he came back with all of the sardonyx, Brother Richard wouldn't be surprised if his Clan made him their leader. In the last year, the Clan had been leaderless and highly disorganized. He would save them all.

He ran along some marked trails, across a few streams, and down some hillsides. While it was dark, he could see well enough to identify the amazingly large field in front of him. Going full out, he charged across the cut grass, enjoying the slight dew on the surface.

"Halt!" came a stern sounding command.

Being in his wolf form, Brother Richard might have ignored the man had he not spotted four dragons rimming the park like area, all of whom were breathing fire. Shit, shit, shit. How in the hell had he not sensed them? He knew: his thoughts had been someplace else—like going home a savior.

Was one of these dragons the animal who'd followed him from the woman's house? Only one way to find out? Shift. If he hadn't been in a large open field, he would have chanced running into the forest. He had the sense that dragons would be fairly useless if they couldn't fly, and Brother Richard was fast.

He shifted. The four dragons followed suit. Okay, that was odd. They were all fully dressed. He however was not. How was that possible?

Brother Richard lifted his chin. "What is the meaning of this? You have no right to stop me. It's a free country." He honestly had no idea if that was true, but the United States was free.

"You are on the King's property. Seize him!"

What? "Wait a minute. I was minding my own business. You can't do this."

Apparently they didn't care. One minute he was facing them, and the next he was grabbed from behind and taken straight upward. Holy shit. As much as Brother Richard wanted to struggle, he feared the monster who had him would let go. A fall from this height might kill him, or at the very least, injure him significantly. He debated shifting back into his wolf form, but the change might also result in the dragon dropping him.

Before he could wrap his head around how all of this had happened, a huge castle appeared. While Brother Richard had traveled in his time and had seen castles in Scotland, none were occupied. Given the amount of lit windows, this one was inhabited. His human instinct told him that this was the King's property they spoke of. If that were true, where the hell was he exactly? Damned if he knew. For a few days now, he had the sneaking suspicion he might be in a realm other than Earth, and that scared him more than he was willing to admit.

The dragon deposited him in front of this massive structure. As soon as his feet touched the ground, the creature holding him shifted into a guard—if his khaki colored uniform was any indication.

"You have this all wrong," Brother Richard said. "I was out for a run. I didn't see any signs that said I was on private property. I apologize. It won't happen again."

The first man grabbed his arm and led him to a large door. "You'll be able to speak with someone tomorrow about your complaint."

Okay, that didn't sound so bad. At least he thought so until this man led him down a series of corridors that had him lost in no time. After what seemed like forever, he'd had it—with the cold, the dampness, and the putrid smell.

Needing to get the hell out of there, Brother Richard shifted and leapt at the guard, ready to rip him apart. He was in mid-air when the guard held out his hand. It was as if Brother Richard hit a wall, causing him to drop to the ground like a stone. What the hell kind of power did this man possess?

The guard watched as Brother Richard scrambled to his feet. He'd be damned if he shifted back. It was bad enough being naked, but he didn't like being treated like a prisoner.

"Come," the guard commanded.

Brother Richard turned around and tried to race back to the entrance, only his legs refused to work. This was ridiculous. What had this man done to him? Deciding he had more control when in his human form, he shifted. "I demand to know what you just did to me."

"Come." With that the guard turned around and continued down the path.

Ass. While Brother Richard believed he could find his way back to the entrance, he doubted they'd let him walk out of there. Most likely those freaky dragons were right outside waiting to tear him apart. Tomorrow, he'd demand to be freed and this guard punished. This lowly man had no respect for anyone.

Chapter Twelve

H OLY CRAP. BROTHER Richard was in jail! A real life, cramped, stinking jail cell—all because he decided to go for a run. There had to be a mistake. When he'd called out to the other prisoners, no one answered. Either he was the only one there, or they had been told not to speak to him. Jerks. Someone would pay for this kind of treatment.

A shuffling noise came toward him. A moment later, a slumped over guard appeared, carrying a tray with some kind of food on it. Brother Richard jumped up from his lumpy bed. "I demand to speak with the person in charge."

He'd never seen this guard before, but the man just stared at him, acting a little daft. Once he placed the tray on the floor and shoved it through the opening, he left.

"Hey, you! I need to talk with you."

Clearly, the man was deaf. When Brother Richard looked at the meal though, it appeared quite appetizing. He picked up the tray and proceeded to eat the whole thing. At least they had the decency to give him some good fare.

Once he finished, he returned the tray to the slot, but then he suddenly had this need to rest. He hadn't slept much if at all last night, so he had no problem lying down. It wasn't as if he had anything else to do.

He awoke to someone slapping his face.

"Wake up, trespasser."

"Huh?" Brother Richard opened his eyes.

He was no longer in his cell but rather in a hallway. Two guards were holding him up. At least someone had dressed him, though he remembered none of it. Pissed at being there at all, Brother Richard attempted to straighten, but his stomach revolted. He wouldn't let them see how weak he was though. Pride made him straighten his shoulders and endure the discomfort.

When he looked around, he was stunned to find he was in a part of the castle that was quite grand. The beamed ceilings had to have been forty feet tall. While the walls were all stone, the coats of armor and lit torches on the walls were impressive.

Only then did he realize his hands were chained in front of him, and there was an additional chain between his feet. "Why am I here?" he asked in his most authoritative tone.

"You are about to meet the man in charge. You are chained because we don't want you to escape."

Given his surroundings, this person was someone special. That put a different light on things. "Why didn't you tell me last night I would be seeing someone so important?"

"We did." They rapped on a magnificent hand-carved wooden door.

"Enter," came the response.

The door opened, and one of the guards pushed him in.

Brother Richard was stunned at not only the room's opulence but with the man in the fine clothes sitting behind a desk. If Brother Richard believed in time travel, he would have pegged this to be somewhere in the seventeen hundreds.

The man in the blue suit, wearing a cravat and more jewelry than Richard had ever seen in his life, stood and walked around his desk. "I've been told you are different."

Different? What did that mean? "If you say so. Are you the king?" Brother Richard asked.

"No. I'm Prince Omar. My father, the king, is ill and is unable to attend this meeting." The prince ran his gaze over Brother Richard's body. "What kind of shifter are you?"

"Wolf."

"But not an ordinary wolf."

He was surprised the prince could sense the Changeling in him. "No. I'm not ordinary at all."

Needing to plea for his release, Brother Richard reached out and touched the man's arm. The prince jerked back as if he'd been burned. "How dare you touch me, you vermin."

What an arrogant prick! "You don't understand."

"I understand perfectly. Where are you from?" the prince asked.

Why did it matter? "Silver Lake, Tennessee."

"Where is that?"

Maybe there was something in the water, because no one seemed to understand anything. "In the U.S." Doofus.

His eyes widened. "You live on Earth? Ah, that explains a lot."

"Just like you," he said without thinking.

Then everything cleared. Holy shit. He was in a different realm, and his gut soured.

The man stepped back around his desk, pulled out his chair, and sat down. "You, my odd little fellow, have no idea where you are. You are on Tarradon, a realm hidden from Earth."

The big swirling hole he'd stepped through must have been a portal to this other place. Holy shit. Before he could truly understand what it all meant, a charge shot through his body, just like it always did when he changed into another person. Only that couldn't be what was happening now. He could only transform into some other being during a red moon, which came about once a month, and he certainly hadn't spotted one last night.

The prince pointed at him. "You! What did you do?"

"Nothing, why?"

The prince stood, but then stopped moving, almost as if he were dizzy. The pompous ass walked over to him, grabbed his arm, and dragged him in front of a mirror.

Brother Richard stared at himself. Holy shit. He looked just like the prince.

"How did you do this?" the prince asked. "I demand you return to your old self."

"I, ah, am not sure what happened." When the prince raised his hand, Brother Richard babbled, "I'll try."

He closed his eyes and focused on returning to his fifty-year-old self. When he was in Silver Lake, he remained looking like the person until the spell wore off, so he wasn't certain he could do what the prince asked of him—but he would attempt to. With a great deal of concentration, a surge of power shot through him once more. When he opened his eyes and checked the mirror, he was back to being Brother Richard Donovan. Phew, that was close.

The prince moved back to his seat and dropped onto the chair—or rather what looked more like a throne. "Guard!" he shouted.

Footsteps sounded and the door burst open. "Yes, your Prince?"

"Unchain this man."

Brother Richard sighed. "Thank you."

The guard unlocked the cuffs on his wrists and around his ankles. Unsure of what came next, he waited for the prince to say something.

"Sit down. We have much to discuss."

IT HAD BEEN close to two weeks since the death of Betty and Henry Tisdale, but Anderson said he was no closer to finding their killer. Knowing this Earthling was still in the realm and could strike at any time unsettled everyone. After what happened to Greer with the dark entity, she was chomping at the bit to find this guy and rid Tarradon of one more evil force that had invaded their realm. If Chelsea, a wolf and dragon shifter, hadn't been five months pregnant, Greer would have suggested she help with the search. Finn was spending his free time looking for the guy but hadn't had any success. Greer was convinced that Blake held the key.

She leaned back against the jewelry counter, wishing Tory worked today. The store had been lacking customers, and there was only so much cleaning and polishing one could do.

Her cell rang, jerking her attention back to the present. It was her brother Griffin. That was a surprise. "Hey. What's up?"

"Anderson has something for us."

Excitement raced through her veins. "Do you know what it is?"

"No, but he's coming over to the conference room in an hour."

That put the meeting during lunch. She had no problem closing the store for that time. "Thanks for letting me know. See you then."

In case the meeting was about the man who had robbed her, she wanted Blake to be there. Now that Greer had more or less moved into Blake's place, her love for him had blossomed. The sex was outrageous, further increasing her belief they'd be mated soon. Now was as good a time as any to include him in every aspect of her life.

With the store devoid of customers, she called him.

"Hey, sexy lady. What's up?"

She chuckled. "Hello, yourself. By any chance do you have say, an hour to spare? Detective Caspian is coming over to SinCas, and I'd like you to be present to hear what he has to say."

Blake said nothing for a few seconds. "What's this about, Greer?" His tone had turned hard.

"I don't know, but I'm suspecting it's about the man who robbed me."

"Then I'll make sure to be there. What time?"

She wanted to discuss something with him first. "Forty minutes?"

"I'll be there."

"Thank you," she said.

She kept herself busy, checking the inventory and making certain the countertop was clean for the hundredth time. When the front door buzzer sounded, she let Blake in. Instantly, her body heated up, and her scales flashed. The broad smile he gave her had her wanting to put the closed sign on the door immediately and drag him into the backroom. If an important meeting wasn't about to occur in twenty minutes, she would have. Instead, she wrapped her arms around his neck and kissed him.

Given anyone on the street could see them helped her rein in her urges. When the kiss turned into roaming hands, they broke apart.

"I don't think you asked me here just to make out, but if you did, I'm game," Blake said. "I thought we had a meeting to go to, or was that a ruse?"

"No, not a ruse, but I want to talk to you first. Let's sit on the sofas." Because there were often bored spouses and children, there was a sitting area near the front.

"What's this about, Greer. You look serious. Is something wrong?"

He couldn't possibly think anything was wrong between them. "Not as far as I'm concerned, but I need to come clean about something."

"You can tell me anything."

Greer believed that. Once they sat next to each other, she inhaled. "I think it's clear that we are meant for each other."

"I totally agree."

She didn't like his pinched brows though. It was as if he was waiting for her to tell him they couldn't be together or something, and that was the furthest from the truth. "Do you know about the Guardians?"

"Everyone knows about them, but no one knows who they are." He clasped her hand. "Do you know?"

"Yes. I'm one of them."

Blake chuckled but then quickly sobered. "You aren't kidding, are you?"

"No." She explained how the Caspians and the Sinclairs were the Guardians. "I needed to tell you because I might be called on to do something at any time."

He tightened his hold. "I don't like the idea of you putting yourself in danger like that."

She figured he'd respond that way. "I've been training to do this since I was young. Don't worry. I might look delicate—or so

VELLA DAY

everyone tells me—but I'm a good fighter, though I'll be the first to admit I'm better in the air than on the ground."

"Maybe you'll just have to show me."

Greer couldn't tell if he was challenging her, or if he was really worried she couldn't handle herself. It didn't matter. She had no problem demonstrating her skills. "I'd love to, but right now we have more pressing issues."

"The visit from Detective Caspian?"

"Yes. We both should know what is going on with this guy. I don't want to have any secrets between us. Besides, I'm thinking with your special skills, you might be able to help."

"Help find this thief?" He shook his head. "I'm not sure how. I lost him once already."

"He will resurface. We're pretty sure he's killed at least two people."

Blake jerked as if she'd slapped him. "When? Tell me what you know."

She gave him a brief rundown of Anderson's theory—aided by Finn's hypothesis—about some rabid werewolf from Earth who needed sardonyx to help keep his Clan alive. "He might be the one responsible for the deaths and the theft."

"That's scary."

"I know, right?" She further explained about the possible portal breach, and how her brother Birk had truly believed he'd spoken with the real Henry Tisdale. "Finn said that these Changelings can touch someone and transform to look like them."

"This is all so incredible, but I don't see any proof that the man who robbed you of the sardonyx lamp is connected to these deaths, other than both involved the same stone."

"Besides the two deaths, another miner was attacked. It's possible the attacker thought he'd killed Gregory Malpan, but he didn't. Mr. Malpan gave us a description of the man. It sounds like he was the same person who came into our jewelry store the day you were in there."

"Was he wearing a hat and a brown suit?"

"No, but the age, height, and weight are the same." The proof sounded weak. "Crap. We have nothing." Greer blew out a breath.

"If it is the same man, I might be able to help."

Greer sat up straighter. "How?"

"I saw the essence trail—for lack of a better phrase—of the man who robbed you. If I run into him again, I might be able to identify him."

Excitement raced through her. "That's fantastic."

He held up a hand. "Trails run cold, and like a smell, it's easy to forget. If I hadn't been so taken with you that day in the store, I would have paid closer attention to the man asking about the sardonyx. All I remember is that I got this evil vibe off of him—one that had a gray tinge to it."

Her pulse rose. "That really helps." Her cell buzzed with a message stating the meeting was about to begin. She showed it to him. "Let's see what Anderson has to say."

"Tell me again why Detective Caspian would come here other than the fact that he is a relative?"

"The police force often needs help dealing with anything related to magic. If the thief is the killer, humans wouldn't stand a chance against him. Anderson often asks for the Guardians' help when dealing with those kind of things."

A small smile lifted his lips. "So that's why your family was so involved when Mange took over my body."

"Yes, and the fact I was attacked."

"Sorry about that."

She sighed and shook her head. "I know you weren't personally responsible."

"Thank you." Blake leaned over in plain sight of those walking by and kissed her.

Lust swamped her, escalating her need. Fortunately, reason intruded before she let her libido take over. "We really need to go." She put the sign on the door stating they were closed but would return shortly. She then escorted Blake to the hallway. "Let's take the stairs."

"You're wearing high heels."

He had no idea that her heels were part of her anatomy. "Not a problem. It's only four flights."

He stopped her. "Are you claustrophobic or something?"

"No." She told him about Mange sabotaging the elevator. "I know it's fixed, but I don't want to take any chances, especially if we have a killer on the lose."

Blake nodded, his eyes shining in appreciation. "I'm glad I'm about to mate with such a hot, sexy, and smart woman."

"Thank you, but you aren't so bad yourself."

Chapter Thirteen

WHEN SHE AND Blake entered the room, Greer wasn't surprised that everyone stopped talking and faced them. After all, Blake was the man who'd kidnapped her. Anderson was speaking with her uncle and dad, while the rest were milling around the coffee station, clearly waiting for them to arrive. Okay. Fine. She and Blake had spent a few extra minutes making out and were late. There was no crime in that. Besides, she was defenseless against Blake's allure.

Tory was there, smiling, while most of the rest were not. "Hi, everyone," Greer said in a rather professional tone. "Most of you know Blake Masters, but what I may not have shared with you yet is that Blake is my mate."

As soon as she said that last word, everyone was all smiles. They rushed up to her, hugged and congratulated her, and then shook Blake's hand and patted him on the back.

"Why didn't you tell us?" her dad asked with obvious joy in his tone.

"Mom knew, but I swore her to secrecy." Okay, Tory knew too, and she suspected Griffin had an idea, but why mention that? "I've been trying to find the right time to tell you all."

Her father smiled. "I'm so happy for you." He turned to Blake. "Welcome to the family, son."

Blake shook his hand. "Thank you, sir."

"Call me Laird."

Uncle Jamison tapped the table. "Congratulations you two, but Anderson is on a tight schedule. We need to get down to business."

Everyone found a seat.

"I'm afraid my search for this elusive Changeling has not produced any viable results," Anderson said. "I was about to put the search on the back burner when a few cases crossed my desk that seemed rather odd."

"Odd?" Declan asked.

"Possibly connected." Anderson nodded at Blake. "When someone broke into Greer's house and stole a sardonyx salt lamp, Blake here was able to note the vehicle's model and the first two digits of the license plate. It was a dark blue Camron. While Blake followed him into the forest, he was unable to pursue him deep into the woods. With that information though, we learned that a car matching that description had recently been stolen. Finding said car parked near a gas station in town two days ago was a surprise however."

"Maybe he realized that Blake saw the type of car he was driving and decided he should steal another vehicle," Greer said.

"That was my thought. That's why I believe he was responsible for the theft of a second car, which was a white Branton."

This guy had already proven that he was a thief, but so far, not that he was a murderer.

"How do you know it's the same guy who stole both the first car and the second one?" Declan asked.

"I'm getting to that. Turns out Gary Hickman is the owner of this Branton. He said his car was stolen when he was getting gas the other night. Just when he'd finished pumping the gas, one of his neighbors arrived on foot." Anderson checked his phone. "A Tom Arlington. For no reason, Tom grabbed Gary, punched him hard enough to flatten him, stole his keys, and then hopped in Gary's car and drove off."

Greer was confused. "What does this have to do with that Changeling person? Gary identified the thief as his neighbor, not some random fifty-year old."

Anderson held up a hand. "That's what I thought until one of my officers spoke with Tom Arlington. At the time of the incident, he was giving a speech to a room full of doctors. I've seen the tape. He couldn't have stolen Gary's car."

"Was Gary confused then about who had decked him and stole his car?" Greer asked.

"He claims he wasn't."

"It was the Changeling, wasn't it?" Blake asked, his lips pursed.

"Most likely, but because I didn't want to jump to any conclusions, I called Finn for more clarification about those werewolf mutants and what they are capable of. I needed to know if they could change other than during a red moon. Considering we don't have red moons on Tarradon, I was hoping he couldn't transform. Finn, please tell everyone what you told me."

Finn nodded. "Mind you, I don't know everything about the abilities of these freaks of nature, but from years of studying them, they could only change into another person roughly once a month. At least that is the case on Earth, but it doesn't mean it's the same on Tarradon."

"Tell me about it," Declan said. "I can personally vouch for the fact that things on Tarradon don't always mirror events on Earth. Look at how going through the portal affected my mate's hormones." He smiled, and the rest of the group chuckled.

Greer had to admit her cousin brought up a good point. The portal had altered more than one woman's chemistry. Chelsea hadn't taken any extra safeguards after passing through it and became fertile almost immediately, despite her precautions on Earth.

Blake raised his hand. "You're saying that this Changeling can turn into another person at will? That he might not need a red moon to do it?" That was really scary.

Finn leaned forward. "It appears that might be the case."

"That really sucks," Blake said.

Everyone nodded. "I've put out an alert for the car, but I can't give them too many details," Anderson said. "Many of my human officers wouldn't understand if I told them the thief might be a fifty-year old man or someone looking totally different."

"That makes our job of finding him almost impossible," Uncle Jamison said.

Anderson flipped through his notes. "It seems so, but I'm sure he'll slip up. In fact, late last night, a convenience store was robbed. I didn't give it much thought since a homicide wasn't involved, but the report I received this morning had the same facts as the car robbery."

"Don't tell me the person caught on camera was someplace else at the time of the theft," Declan said.

Anderson pointed a finger at him. "Give the man a gold star. This Changeling isn't being very smart about who he turns into though. This time, he touched a clergyman. The priest claimed to have been asleep all night, and I tend to believe him."

Greer sucked in a breath. "You would think this Changeling dude would target some of our poor who might have a reason to steal."

"You would think."

"The Changelings are very arrogant," Finn said. "He'll believe he is above getting caught. If he does, all he'd have to do is touch a guard and demand he be released from prison. He could even turn into Anderson and fool us all."

This was beyond scary. "Does this Changeling have the same memories as this person?" Greer asked.

Finn shook his head. "Not that we've ever learned about."

"Good. If we find there are two Andersons, we can ask him questions that only you could answer."

Anderson nodded. "Let's hope it doesn't come to that, but if you suspect something is off, we could use a password, like..." He waved his tablet. "Tablet."

The group mumbled. "We need to hope the Changeling isn't one of your officers," Greer said.

"Then there would be two of them," Anderson shot back. "I'm sure I can ask about a case the officer was on. I'd be able to spot the

Changeling immediately."

That was assuming the Changeling didn't kill the officer first, but Greer decided not to belabor the point.

Birk slapped the table and sighed. "That's why when I questioned who I thought was Henry Tisdale, this imposter hemmed and hawed. He knew nothing about the real Henry's life."

The group spoke up at once, until Anderson held up his hand. "That is good news for us. It also means that because he may not have a real understanding of the portal system he could end up in Cargonia or some other realm. It's not like the portals are labeled. It's up to the Guardians to make sure the people end up in the right place. This Changeling might not be aware of that."

A few people chuckled.

"Anything else, Anderson?" her uncle asked, obviously trying to keep the meeting moving forward.

"Yes. I forgot to mention there was a third robbery in the Bentwood district last night. The owners came home in the middle of the robbery and recognized the thief as their neighbor. Before you ask, that neighbor was able to provide proof that he wasn't involved. Lucky for them, the Bentwood house had security cameras. Parked nearby was Gary Hickman's Branton again. That leads me to believe the same person is doing all of this."

"What would you like us to do?" Greer's dad asked, finally chiming in.

"Keep your eyes and ears open."

Blake looked around. "I might be able to help."

Everyone swiveled toward him. "How?" Anderson asked.

He explained to the rest of the group about his unique talent of being able to identify a person's essence trail. "Mind you, it doesn't last long, but when I was following this creep to the forest, his trail was faint but unique. I can't be positive, but it could have matched the guy who came into the jewelry store asking for something with sardonyx."

"You said you could help. What can you do?" Anderson asked.

VELLA DAY

"I can go into the forest and see if I can pick up the trail. It's a long shot, but I have nothing to lose other than time."

"That would be great. Keep us posted. If there is another theft, I might be calling on you to see if you can pick up a more recent trail."

"Perfect."

Greer was so proud of the way Blake had stepped up to help. They spent another few minutes discussing what role the other Guardians could play. Needless to say, they were aware of the need to be more vigilant. Thankfully, they could tell a wolf shifter from a bear shifter from a dragon shifter. Whether they could sense a Changeling from a regular wolf shifter was anyone's guess, though the Guardians did possess magical abilities few others did.

Once the room emptied out, Greer and Blake took the stairs down to the jewelry shop. The moment they stepped inside the store, Blake clasped her shoulders, leaned over, and kissed her. Wild spikes of joy shot up her spine. Would her body ever stop reacting so intensely to this man? Hopefully not.

When she caught sight of two people grinning through the window, she broke contact. "Any more of this insane kissing and I'll need to take off the rest of the day to make love with you back at your place."

"Wouldn't that be nice, but I too have to get back to work. How about I pick you up at five? I trust you'll want to stop back at your townhouse for some hiking gear. Then we can look for this werewolf scoundrel."

"Sounds good, but do you really think you can pick up his trail after all this time?"

"Not if he hasn't been back there recently. I'd go right now, but I'm kind of on shaky grounds with corporate as it is. They weren't thrilled with my arrest, even though they said they understood it wasn't my fault."

"You never said anything."

Blake dragged a knuckle down her cheek. "I knew it would blow over. If I were positive we could find this guy, I would go now." He

106

held up a finger. "I forgot to ask. Did Anderson mention anything about finding any evidence of this mutant werewolf at any of the hotels? He might not even be in the woods anymore."

She had to think for a minute. "I don't think so, but it's always possible the Changeling will touch some guest and then stay in a different hotel under that person's name for a day or so."

"Shit. I hadn't thought of that, but if that is the case, he'd need to pay in cash. He couldn't have gotten a credit card at our bank without a lot of identification."

"I'll ask Anderson if anyone had their license or credit cards stolen," Greer said.

He tapped her nose. "I think you should be a detective."

She chuckled and then ran a hand down his chest. "We could open a detective agency together, you know."

"As much as I'd like that, I don't want you to be in any more danger than you already are."

She appreciated his overprotective nature, but it was unnecessary. "You don't have to worry about me. If you recall, I was going to show you a thing or two about fighting. It will put your mind at ease, I promise."

He laughed. "I'd like to see that."

"You're on. See you at five."

"At five."

BLAKE WAS STILL reeling from learning that Greer was a Guardian. Being in the room with so many others like her had been a bit intimidating at first, but their focus and desire to help others showed how approachable and decent they were.

After the meeting, Blake wanted to do his part more than anything. This creep from Earth was a thief at best. Whether he'd killed anyone, he couldn't say, but if Detective Caspian believed he was a suspect, then Blake would consider him dangerous.

Blake debated telling Greer that he wanted to go into the woods by himself to search for this person of interest since he didn't like the idea of someone as classy as Greer tromping around the woods, but knowing her, she'd tell him she was coming regardless of what he said. She'd better be as well trained as she claimed, or he'd live in fear for the rest of his life.

If they ran into that creepy werewolf though, what was the worst that could happen? Blake could shoot some fire at the fur ball and end his pathetic life. Too bad Blake wasn't a cold-blooded killer. Otherwise the problem would be easily solved. If this Changeling turned out to be merely a thief, he didn't deserve to die—especially by burning to death.

Blake's immediate concern was that being around Greer would diminish his ability to follow this man's essence trail. Like he'd told the others, the trail from when the man robbed Greer would be long gone, but if he spotted him again, Blake should be able to identify him.

As soon as the bank closed, Blake headed up to his apartment to change before picking up Greer. He just hoped she owned boots—ones without high heels.

At five, he drove to her shop situated at the base of the SinCas building. To his surprise, Greer was waiting outside for him. Once again, she pulled open the car door and hopped in, not giving him the chance to show his more chivalrous side.

When she closed the door, he leaned over and kissed her. While he understood it would be difficult to stop once he touched her, he needed the rush from the contact. She leaned back and smiled, and his heart melted. Greer was truly his mate. "How did your day go?" he asked.

"A little slow. I couldn't wait to see you again."

She was the sweetest woman. "Me too."

After they arrived at her house so she could change, Greer placed a hand on his arm. "How about staying in the car?"

He hadn't expected that. "Why?"

"Why? Because if I get you anywhere near a bed, I'll have to make love with you, and I think it will be easier to spot this guy while it's light."

He grinned. Greer always said the best things. "Go."

To his delight, she returned in under ten minutes, which for Greer might have been a new record. She opened the passenger side door and leaned in. "We aren't flying?"

"No. We have too much area to cover once we reach the dense canopy of trees. Having a car will be more efficient."

She slid in. "Works for me."

The trip to the forest entrance didn't take long. During that time though, Greer said little—probably because he'd explained that remembering the essence trail of every person required concentration.

Once they entered the road covered in trees, Blake slowed. "The last reported car stolen was a white Branton. Keep your eyes peeled for it on the right, and I'll look on the left."

"Will do," she said with a lot of excitement, implying she had been raised to do this.

Blake drove slow enough to give them time to spot something. They were halfway through the forest when Greer pointed and shouted, "That looks like the car."

He eased off to the side and stopped. "Let's check it out."

As soon as they approached the vehicle, Blake noted a faint trail swirling around it. "This is his."

"You can see his essence coming off it?"

"Yes."

"Can you tell where he went?"

He gave her a self-satisfied smile. "I can. Let's go catch us a thief."

Because Blake was the one who could detect the trail, he led, checking frequently to make sure she was doing okay hiking over the rather rough terrain. They'd agreed to keep talking to a minimum, because voices traveled far in the forest. They'd gone about twenty minutes when he stopped.

Greer stepped next to him. "What is it?" she whispered.

"I sense a shifter. He's moving through the forest."

She said nothing for a few seconds. "I hear him now too. What's the plan?"

He turned around. "I don't feel right rushing in and outright killing him. More importantly, I can't be certain he killed anyone."

"I bet he has, but I understand your caution. Can't you tell if his electric aura thing matches the one you saw before?"

"Yes. It's definitely him, but until we know for sure he's a murderer, he doesn't deserve to die for stealing a lamp."

"Maybe not. What do you want to do then?"

Greer was the Guardian, but he appreciated her asking for his opinion. "Let's move a little closer, but not so close that he spots or senses us. If he does, and then shifts into his wolf form, we'll be forced to burn him."

"It would be nice if Finn were here. He's a wolf shifter as well as a dragon shifter. He could take down this guy."

Take down or kill? "I think it would be smart to leave the final capture to the cops." He might have had a different opinion if her cousin wasn't the lead on this case. It didn't matter Blake wanted to destroy the man with his bare hands worse than anything.

She nodded, and they moved as quietly as possible down the trail. Some noise sounded to his right, and out of the corner of his eye, an essence trail floated by. Blake stopped. "It's him," he whispered, wishing they could communicate telepathically.

As if the Changeling sensed them, leaves crunched and then an animal scurried away. Damn. Neither of them would be any good in their dragon form. As a human, his only weapon was fire. Even at that, his aim and ability to shoot far using his arm when partially shifted wasn't the best. Not to mention, they certainly didn't need to start a forest fire.

"He got away," she said, sounding a bit dejected.

"It seems so."

Greer grabbed his shoulder. "Let's at least see if we can find where he's staying."

"I doubt he has a tent. He's a wolf."

"He might have his clothes stashed nearby. Knowing the location of his hideout would be valuable information to Anderson. Please?"

He couldn't handle her look of disappointment. "We can check it out and maybe even figure out a way to mark the site for the cops to find."

She smiled. "You are a good team player."

For now. If he came head to head with the guy without Greer being near, all bets were off.

Chapter Fourteen

THE NEXT TWO days were rather tense. Blake really wanted to locate this Changeling, because the cops hadn't succeeded despite being given a detailed description of his last known location. Detective Caspian said all had been quiet on the crime front too. In fact, no one had reported any strange events involving a doppelganger.

At first Blake thought this guy might have hightailed it back to Earth, but then Greer said that when she checked everyone going to Earth had been personally known to the Guardians. They'd even called each home to make sure that person wasn't there and at the portal at the same time. All Blake could do now was wait.

He'd just stepped out of the shower after a long day at work when Greer popped her head into the bathroom. He loved how her eyes turned that pretty purple every time he was naked—or kissing her.

She covered her eyes. "I can't look."

He chuckled. "Why not? Afraid you'll have to ravish me?" Blake grabbed a towel to dry off.

She opened them up. "Yes, and Kaleena just called and asked if I'd come over. She's not feeling all that well and wants some company as well as my healing hands."

"Then by all means go." He understood how much Greer worried about her two pregnant friends. While he'd yet to meet Kaleena, she was Finn's mate. The other woman, Chelsea, who was even further along than Kaleena, was Declan's mate.

Blake didn't want to become distracted imagining how wonderful his life would be when he and Greer had children of their own, so he wrapped the towel around his waist and stepped past her into their bedroom.

"What are you going to do tonight?" she asked as she trailed after him. "I hate for you to be home all alone."

"Actually, I was thinking of heading over to the Wing's Bar to chat with Finn. The more I learn about the Changelings and their habits, the better chance I have of finding him."

"That sounds great. I won't be gone too long, I hope."

"Don't rush; if you're not home when I get back from the bar, I'll watch some TV, but if I fall asleep just get me up when you come in."

She grinned. "From the looks of what's happening under your towel, I'd say something is already up."

He laughed. "Go."

The temptation to sweep her off her feet and feast on her was strong, but Blake resisted. Her scent alone was messing with his cock, his scales, and everything in between.

It took at least an hour after Greer left for his libido to calm. At around eight thirty, Greer texted to say she would be staying with Kaleena for a little bit longer, and she hoped he would be okay. Blake chuckled and immediately texted back saying he was about to head out to the Wings Bar and not to worry about him.

The bar wasn't far, so he decided to walk there. As he neared the entrance, a familiar light floated by. It appeared to be similar to that of the Changeling thief, but Blake couldn't be positive since so many people were driving by and walking down the sidewalk. Essences, he'd learned, tended to blend together with time.

Keeping his attention focused, he stepped inside, and when he didn't sense the man's aura in there, he relaxed. As he'd planned, Blake sat at the bar. When Finn was free, the two chatted about what the Changelings were like back on Earth and how when they shifted, it tore apart their clothes. It was why shifters undressed before transforming.

"I'm glad that doesn't happen here," Blake said.

"No kidding. It took me some time to get used to remaining dressed."

Finn then regaled him with a story about his brother Rye and his mate Izzy who'd been stalked by a Changeling—one who had bound her powers for a while. It was rather scary stuff.

After Blake finished his second beer, the heat and the noise began to irritate him. Usually, he was one to go out and have a good time, but ever since he'd met his mate, his priorities had changed. He found peace and solace staying home with Greer. She was so interesting that he wanted to spend a lifetime learning about her.

"Another beer?" Finn asked as he polished the counter in front of Blake after removing his empty glass.

His cell chimed. "No, I'm good. That's Greer. She's heading home now. I guess your mate is doing okay. Thanks for the company."

"You bet. Stop by anytime!"

As Blake stepped outside, the essence trail he'd sensed on his way in was now a faint hint of light. He shook his head, ready for some hard loving with Greer.

BLAKE'S BUZZING CELL phone jarred him awake. The bedside clock told him it wasn't even six a.m. Who the hell was calling so early? It wasn't a bank alert because no red flashing sign appeared.

Because Greer was sound asleep next to him, he grabbed his phone, walked out of the bedroom, and closed the door.

The caller ID said it was Finn, which he found odd. "Hey, what's up?" Blake asked, keeping his voice low.

"It's Kaleena. She's been arrested."

Blake grabbed the kitchen island chair and sat down. "What are you talking about?"

"Anderson came to the condo about an hour ago, knocked on

our door, and said Kaleena needed to come down to the station." The sounds in the background indicated Finn was there now.

Nothing made any sense. "Arrested for what?"

"Murder."

He'd not met Kaleena, but Greer was very attached to her cousin. "Hold on. Murder? That's crazy. Greer was with her all last night. When did this happen?"

"At around eleven thirty last night."

Shit. Greer was home by then. "Are you at the station now?"

"Yes."

"What can we do?"

"Can you and Greer come down here now? I'm hoping both of your testimonies will help."

"Of course. We'll be right over."

As soon as he disconnected, Blake raced back into the bedroom. "Greer, honey, wake up."

She opened her eyes, and when she smiled, his dragon went wild. As much as he'd love nothing more than a repeat of last night's lovemaking, Kaleena needed them. "You need to get dressed. Kaleena's been arrested for murder."

Greer bolted upright. "What!?"

"Finn just called. I don't know much, but we need to get down to the station. I'll explain what I know on the way."

As if he'd told her the building was on fire, Greer tossed on a pair of jeans and a top in record time. She actually beat him getting dressed. They then rushed to the rooftop, shifted, and flew to the station. The parking lot out back was mostly empty, giving them space to land. After they were on the ground, they shifted and then jogged around to the front entrance of the police station.

"I can't believe this. Does Anderson know?" she asked.

"Anderson arrested her."

"That's ridiculous. He has to know Kaleena would never kill anyone unless it was a matter of life and death," she said.

"I'm sure he knows she didn't do it, but he must have some

evidence to the contrary or he wouldn't have taken her in. He's just doing his job."

She speared him with a rather ugly look. He of all people understood that what Anderson believed and what he did were often different. The detective went by the law and then figured out the truth.

They rushed inside. Finn was pacing in front of Anderson's desk. As soon as he saw them, he rushed up to them. "Thanks for coming."

"Of course. How is Kaleena?" Greer asked, sounding in pain herself.

"Not good. The baby is acting up. Being falsely accused hasn't been easy for her, but if she endured all that time in the castle prison, she'll get through this."

During her capture, according to the story Greer told him, Kaleena hadn't been pregnant at the time. It would be different now, but he said nothing.

Greer nodded. "On the bright side, she doesn't have to contend with a dark lighter trying to steal her light."

"True."

Anderson came toward them. "Thanks for coming in. Let's find a more private place for me to take your statement."

Finn must have mentioned the possibility of the Changeling's involvement. Blake and Greer followed Finn and Anderson down a darkly lit corridor. This place gave Blake the creeps, mostly because it was filled with bad memories of his incarceration.

"Let's step in here," Anderson said.

The room was better lit and cleaner than the interrogation room where he was first taken to, but it was still small and oppressive. They all sat down.

"Blake, Finn said you went to the Wing's Bar last night. Tell me what time you arrived and when you left," Anderson said.

He hadn't mentioned anything about spotting the essence trail to Finn, but maybe Finn remembered seeing the guy who everyone believed was the Changeling. "I went to the bar around eight thirty. Right before I stepped inside, I thought I saw the same light signature as the man who stole the lamp from Greer's house. It seemed to be the same as the one Greer and I located in the forest."

"Why didn't you tell me?" Finn asked with a sharp edge to his voice.

Blake held up a hand. "I couldn't be sure it was him. There were a lot of people milling about that caused their trails to blend with his. To be honest, I didn't think any more about it when I didn't see any evidence of it inside the bar, though that's to be expected given how many people were in there." Blake leaned on his elbows. "Did you spot someone who could have been a Changeling?" he asked Finn.

Finn blew out a breath. "I can't say for sure. It was a busy night. If I focused on all of the shifter signatures, I'd forget orders. Were there werewolves in the bar? Sure. Was one a Changeling? I can't swear to it."

Finn's outburst a moment ago had completely defused.

Anderson turned to Greer. "What time were you with Kaleena?"

"I think I got there about seven and left a little before ten."

"Kaleena said someone who looked like me visited shortly after that," Finn said to the group.

Blake hadn't heard about this. "Someone who looked like you?"

"Yes. I was still at the bar when some lookalike used the eye scanner and entered our condo."

Greer sucked in a breath. "Kaleena didn't know it wasn't you?"

"She said I rushed in, gave her a quick hug, changed my stained shirt, and rushed out."

Something seemed fishy. "You two are mates. How did she not know it wasn't you? Wouldn't she have sensed the sexual pull was missing?" Blake asked. He'd never be fooled if a Greer lookalike approached him. He doubted a Changeling could pull that off.

Finn shrugged. "Remember, Kaleena is going through a hard time with the baby. Not only does she have morning sickness, she often isn't feeling well at night—like what happened last night. It's not like I haven't rushed home before in the middle of a shift. She probably was just tired and didn't think anything of it."

"What about the security guard at the entrance to your condo? Was this person able to fool him too?" Blake asked.

Anderson nodded. "I spoke with him. He said this Finn impersonator smiled like he always did but that he didn't address him by name, which Edward thought was odd. Since Finn seemed to be in a hurry to get upstairs, he didn't push it or give it a second thought."

"And I suppose instead of Finn returning a few minutes later, Kaleena came down the stairs instead?" Blake asked.

Finn's eyes lit up. "You're right. My lookalike couldn't pretend to be me returning for the rest of my shift and be Kaleena at the same time."

Anderson leaned back in his seat. "I hadn't thought of that. Good job. I'm betting the Changeling had no idea Kaleena was pregnant and probably wouldn't leave late at night."

"If I had been the intruder—which Blake will attest to that I was not—I would have gone with her if she had been called out on an emergency."

"I'm going to call the judge and see about getting Kaleena released."

"She'll do that?" Greer asked. Her voice shook slightly.

"I'm hoping so. It will be hard to explain what a Changeling is capable of, but I'll do my best. Thank goodness this judge is a dragon shifter herself."

"In the meantime, may I see Kaleena?" Greer asked. "I might be able to help with the morning sickness."

Finn reached across the table and placed a hand on hers. "Thank you."

Anderson pushed back his chair. "I don't see why not, but give me a second to call the judge first." He stepped out of the room. When he returned, he was smiling. "The judge is letting her go for now, but she asked that Kaleena stay at the condo until we resolve this."

"She's under house arrest?" Finn asked.

"Not quite. She feels if Kaleena was a target once, she might be a target again. I suggest you two work something out between you and the security guards—a special code word—so he can tell it's you."

Finn nodded. "This is a nightmare, but we'll do whatever it takes to keep Kaleena safe. She may balk, but I'll convince her to stay put. She can work from home if need be."

After all of the paperwork was signed, and Kaleena was released, she rushed into Finn's embrace, making Blake want to take Greer in his own arms and make sure she came to no harm.

"Let me make sure your baby is okay," Greer said, placing a healing hand on Kaleena's stomach. Seconds later, color returned to Kaleena's face, and the worry lines around her eyes disappeared. Greer was truly a miracle worker.

"Call me if you aren't feeling well, okay?" Greer asked.

"I will, thanks." Kaleena hugged her.

As soon as Finn and Kaleena left, Blake needed something to eat. He wrapped an arm around Greer's waist and led her outside. "What do you say to some coffee—or in your case a tea—and a pastry at Angelique's Coffee Shop?"

She smiled for the first time this morning. "Sounds divine. We need to figure out how to get this guy."

Blake was afraid she'd say that, but given she was a Guardian, he didn't want anyone else by his side. "Works for me."

Chapter Fifteen

B ROTHER RICHARD WAS positive he'd pulled off the murder of the century. Kaleena—the woman he was sent to discredit—never suspected a thing. He had to admit luck was on his side when he'd entered the condo under the pretense of needing to change his shirt. Apparently, this wasn't the first time Finn McKinnon had spilled a drink on himself. Brother Richard had almost blown it though when he wasn't sure where the bedroom was located. Thankfully, an open door revealed an unmade bed, making it easy to identify.

The quick hug he'd given her upon entering enabled him to change from Finn to Kaleena as soon as he left. The only slight snafu was the damn guard who'd asked him—or rather Kaleena—a few questions about what she was doing out so late at night without Finn, but Brother Richard had an answer ready. He told the guard that one of her friends needed her.

After that, it was easy. With so many people milling about the town, all he had to do was find some human who was in the wrong place at the wrong time and stab her. Sure, she cried out, but when he clamped a hand over her mouth and nose for a few minutes, she settled down and died. The hardest part had been finding a location with street cameras where no other passersby were about. He wanted the world to know that the great Kaleena Sinclair was a murderer without him being caught red handed.

After the victorious attack, Brother Richard decided to spend the night in the forest even though he'd managed to lift a few Denlars from the woman's purse. The money would be better spent eating a fabulous meal in town tomorrow when everyone would be gossiping about Kaleena's arrest.

As he neared the forest, he went past the path to his old campground that had been compromised when the jewelry lady—who he believed the blonde called Greer—and her male companion had found it. Thankfully, they didn't notice where he'd buried that sardonyx lamp. Even if they had, it wouldn't have mattered. Prince Omar had promised him all the sardonyx he wanted after his mission was complete.

Once he gathered a suitcase full of the precious gem from his gracious host, he'd be on his way back to Earth where his fellow Changelings would hail him as their new leader.

Life couldn't be any better.

BROTHER RICHARD'S EMOTIONAL high was short-lived however, when two Royal thugs invaded his new campsite the next day. While he was still upset at the intrusion and about the fact the prince refused to let him stay in style at the castle, if Prince Omar wanted to bestow jewels on him sooner rather than later, that was fine by him.

"How did you find me?"

"Prince Omar wants to see you now," was all one of them would say.

"I trust he is pleased that the Sinclair woman is in jail?" Brother Richard asked. No surprise neither of the damn guards answered this question either. That was okay. He didn't need anything from them—only his gems from the prince.

"Follow us."

After traipsing through the forest for fifteen minutes, they emerged onto the large field where he'd first encountered the dragons. His two escorts shifted into their dragon form. Brother Richard thought they'd take off and he'd have to find the prince on his own, but apparently that wasn't the plan. A few seconds later, one of the black-scaled dragons swooped toward him and unceremoni-ously picked him up. Brother Richard knew not to struggle or chance falling. He doubted there would come a time when he was used to this crude form of transportation.

When they arrived at the castle, he was deposited rather abruptly on the ground. Both dragons shifted and were still fully clothed. Envy slashed through him. Brother Richard wished he had that ability.

"Follow us," came the command from one of the dragons.

This time, instead of traveling down a long dark and twisted corridor like the first time he'd come, they entered by the main entrance—an entrance fit for a king. About time they realized his worth. When they came to the door where the prince resided, the guard knocked and announced that the wolf from Earth was there.

Brother Richard spun to face them. "Wolf from Earth indeed. I'll have you know that I am Brother Richard, the future leader of the Changeling Clan in Silver Lake, Tennessee."

"Whatever." He motioned for Richard to enter.

Asshole.

Prince Omar had a scowl that looked like it would be impossible to erase. He stood and pushed back his chair. "You failed."

Brother Richard was stunned. "I beg your pardon, your high-ness." He wasn't sure how to address the prince, but he wanted to show some respect. "You asked me to make sure that Kaleena Sinclair either ended up dead or landed in jail for the rest of her life. Last time I checked, she was in jail for murder."

"Correction. She *was* in jail. While I don't have all of the infor-mation, apparently she was released due to a lack of evidence."

Brother Richard almost foamed at the mouth. "That's preposter-ous. I had to go to great lengths to look like her. While in her form, I killed someone in view of the cameras. I don't know what more I could have done."

"Apparently, they figured out it wasn't her. I want you to return to Earth immediately and never come back. Refuse, and I'll throw you in the dungeon and leave you there for the rest of your miserable life."

The temptation to shift into his wolf form and tear out the prince's throat was strong. Too bad this Omar dude was also probably a dragon shifter. Fire scared Richard. Heat did terrible things to the skin.

Brother Richard lifted his chin. "What about my sardonyx? I did as you asked. I can't help that the police here are incompetent."

"You are the incompetent one. I'm not giving you anything. Now go." The man puffed out his chest, and Brother Richard had to inhale deeply to keep his heart from sending him into cardiac arrest.

He didn't know if he could get through the portal. "I will make it up to you. What if I do something to Greer Caspian? I know she's not a Sinclair, but they are related."

"Get out! Guards?"

Shit. Did he get her last name wrong? "Wait! There must be something I can do." Brother Richard hated sounding weak, but he'd not been given a fair deal.

The same two guards returned and dragged him out before he was able to explain anything else to the prince. With their hands tight on his arms, they practically carried him down the corridor.

As soon as they reached the outside, one of the guards shifted into his dragon form. This time the harsh grab and go was expected. The large dragon flew fairly close to the ground and then set him down at the entrance to the forest. He shifted and faced him. "Don't return or you will be killed," the guard announced.

Before Brother Richard could respond, the man returned to his dragon form and took off. Shit. He couldn't wait to leave Tarradon. But he wouldn't leave right away—not before he took care of one other thing.

NORMALLY, GREER WOULD have gone back home with Kaleena to

make sure she was okay, but her cousin insisted she was fine. She'd even promised to call Angelique later. The white entity had put a magical protective sac around the baby and was on Tarradon by Fate's decree to make sure all of the Guardians' children thrived. If Kaleena became ill, she assured her Angelique would help.

"I hope you feel better," Greer said as she waved goodbye to her cousin.

Kaleena blew her a kiss.

Greer and Blake then walked over to Angelique's Coffee Shop. Greer had hoped to speak to Angelique about what happened, but apparently, they'd just missed her. Greer could only hope she was on her way to visit Kaleena.

Blake ordered a black coffee and a pastry, while she wanted something to help calm her. "I'll have a peach tea and one of those strawberry roll ups," she said, pointing to one of the pastries in the display case.

"We'll bring it right over."

Once they were seated, she leaned forward. "What is your plan?"

"My plan?"

"To find this Changeling. I know the cops are looking for him, but you have the best chance of doing that. Only you can see his essence trail."

"True. I was thinking we should give the cops one more day before we do another search."

"Do you think he'll still be where we found him?" Greer asked.

"Honestly? No. He would have figured out that someone found his secret hiding place. He did run off, after all."

Blake was good at shooting holes in her theories. "Then we'll have to do a more thorough search of the area. Expand where we look."

"That's a good idea," he said.

Their drinks and pastries arrived.

After she finished her amazing sweet pastry, Greer washed it down with her now slightly cooled tea. "Do you want to go after work to look for him?" she asked.

His smile was brief. "Like I said, I think we should wait a day. I get the sense the cops don't like a lot of interference."

"Fine. One day. Then tomorrow, after I get off work, we'll do our thing."

"Perfect. Now, don't get me wrong, I'm excited to capture this creep and end all of the misery as much as you are, but I'm not sure how we can accomplish it even if we locate him. While we can kill him by setting him on fire, that's not my style," Blake said. "I say we do our best to send him to jail unharmed, though I too am uncertain how to do that, especially if he shifts into his wolf form."

She nodded. "If this werewolf becomes involved with kidnapping a mate, then we could ask the Four Sisters of Fate for help. From what I've heard though, they have their hands full right now. Not long ago, the sisters took their annual, two-week vacations to different places, and now each sister has returned home after finding her very own mate."

"You'll have to fill me in on them sometime."

"I will."

Blake polished off the rest of his coffee. "Let's hope your cousin Anderson and his men can perform a miracle."

"Fingers crossed." He raised his brows, acting as if he'd never heard of that expression. "Chelsea uses it all the time. It means you wish that person good luck."

"I see. Ready?" Blake asked. "I need to get to work."

"So do I."

They slipped out the back entrance, shifted, and flew back to his apartment on top of the bank. Once inside, they both changed into their work attire. After they kissed goodbye, they headed off to their own jobs. Leaving Blake each morning was becoming more and more difficult. Greer just wanted to spend the day holding and kissing him. Okay, she wanted to do a little more than that, but they did have to earn a living.

The morning was rather routine, but after lunch, her cell rang. It was her brother Griffin again. "Hey," she said.

"I need your help." He sounded scared.

"What happened?"

"It's Danita. She was attacked by what looks like a wolf shifter. She managed to call me before she passed out. I located her and took her to the safe house. Can you meet us there?"

"Sure. It's Tory's day off, but I'll ask her to cover for me. I'll be there as soon as I can."

Danita had been injured? Holy crap. The woman had been through so much already. First, the Royals had held her hostage in their prison alongside of Kaleena. Even more damaging to her psyche was that she had been subjected to the dark lighter Sanditra for weeks on end. Now apparently, some wolf had attacked her—possibly the same one who was killing and stealing. Danita might never recover emotionally.

Greer called Tory to ask if she could cover for her after explaining why she couldn't man the store.

"Of course. You go. I'll be there in a few. Please give Danita my best. I can't believe she has to suffer another setback."

"I know. She's still in therapy from her incarceration months ago."

After thanking her cousin profusely, Greer rushed up to the rooftop. Once in the open, she took off, and arrived at the Sinclair Mines in no time. As soon as she landed, she shifted and raced into the underground bunker. Not sure where Griffin had Danita, she called out. "Griffin? Where are you?"

The last door on the right opened. "In here," he said.

From the look on his face, the situation was dire. "What happened exactly?" she asked.

"I'm not totally sure. Danita called and said that a wolf had attacked her. She told me where she was, but by the time I found her, she'd passed out and has yet to regain consciousness. I called a doctor who cleaned and bandaged her wounds, but she's not showing any improvement."

The pain and caring in his eyes proved to her how important Danita was to him. He had been the one to care for her after Birk's mate had freed Danita from that horrible castle cell. Greer sensed that Griffin wanted to do more for Danita, but the white lighter was keeping her distance from him.

"Why don't you wait outside so I can do my healing magic?" Greer said.

"Do you want me to call Declan to help you?" he asked.

Their cousin was also a powerful healer, but the two of them had slightly different skills. "Let's not bother him yet. Let me try first."

He nodded. "I'll be in the kitchen."

As soon as her overly anxious brother left, she pulled up a chair and sat next to Danita. Greer placed a hand on the woman's shoulder. "Danita, can you hear me?"

The lovely white lighter didn't respond, but from the way she was thrashing about, she was working hard to regain consciousness. Not wanting Danita to suffer further, Greer closed her eyes and concentrated on sending her light and heat into her patient as she said her special chant. Dark energy rose up inside Danita and nearly burned Greer's hands, but she held tight, forcing this new evil from the injured woman's body.

Danita groaned. Greer opened her eyes and repeated the healing chant once more. Right before Greer's eyes, some of the smaller, uncovered wounds began to heal, and even the color of her pale skin improved. Danita's breathing slowed, and then her body went limp.

Greer stroked her heated forehead, waiting for it to cool. She wasn't sure how long she sat there until finally Danita opened her eyes.

Too bad her eyes widened as she tried to sit up. They'd met several times, so it wasn't as if she didn't know who Greer was.

"It's okay, Danita. You're safe. The wolf is gone."

Danita looked around. "Where's Griffin?"

From the way her brows pinched and her breaths suddenly increased, she was worried about him. Interesting. "He's in the kitchen. I'll get him if you want."

Greer thought she'd tell her not to bother, but Danita nodded.

Greer found Griffin sitting at the kitchen table holding a coffee cup in his hands, staring off into space. As soon as she stepped closer, he shoved back his chair and jumped up. "How is she?"

"Easy there. She'll be fine, but she's asking for you."

The light in his eyes brightened. He set his cup on the table. "Did she say anything?"

Greer held in a laugh. "Not yet. Maybe she wants to tell us both at the same time."

When they entered the room, Danita was running her fingers over the bandages on her arms. She looked up and almost smiled.

"Thank you for saving me," she said to Griffin. Danita looked over at Greer. "Did you heal me?"

"A doctor cleaned and bandaged your arms, but I added a bit of magic to speed up the healing process."

Griffin rushed over to the bed, sat down, and picked up her hand. "How are you feeling?"

"From almost coming back from the dead, quite well, thanks to you and Greer. Where are we?"

"A safe place. Don't worry, no wolf can get to you here." She sighed. "Can you tell me what happened?" he asked.

Danita rubbed her head. "I just started having these premonitions. They just come out of the blue. It's not like I can summon them or anything."

"What are they about?" Griffin asked, keeping his voice soft and reassuring.

"This time, I had the sense that an evil force was following me. I know that sounds ridiculous, because the only evil person interested in me—Sanditra—is dead."

"Maybe not. And I'm not talking about that terrible dark entity who attacked a lot of people recently either."

She shivered. "I thought it was dead."

"Let's just say he's gone forever, but there might be another being here now."

She sucked in a breath. "Who?"

Griffin gave her a brief rundown of the Changeling and what he'd done.

Greer sat on the chair. "Where were you when you sensed this new force?" Greer asked.

"I'd come from a therapy session with Dr. Aminor." She looked up at Griffin. "You know how the woods settle my soul?" He nodded. "I headed to the forest to gain a little perspective on things."

"It helps me too."

His lips turned up, and Greer could have sworn it was with love. Holy shit. Her stoic brother only focused on work and nothing else, but apparently Danita had caught his fancy—or was it more than that?

"Anyway, I parked at one of their picnic spots along the roadside. That's when I heard something rather large running in the woods and sensed this evil."

"You can sense evil that easily?" Greer asked.

"I never used to be able to, but after being incarcerated for so long in the Royal dungeon and subjected to that terrible dark lighter, I can."

"You said you were attacked by a wolf. By any chance did it have red eyes?" Greer asked.

Danita lifted up on her elbows. "Yes! How did you know?"

She filled in the rest of the blanks about this werewolf that Griffin had omitted—such as the color of his eyes.

"He's from Earth?" Danita asked.

"We believe so."

"Why would he attack me?"

"That's what I'm going to find out," Greer said.

Chapter Sixteen

After QUESTIONING DANITA for a while longer, Greer left her in the care of Griffin. Danita's wounds had almost completely healed, and Greer suspected her protective brother would let her return home soon.

The big news Danita had revealed was too important to hold back. Because it was a little after five when she returned to town, Tory had already locked up the store. Yes, she and Blake had decided to give Anderson another day to search, but this Changeling's essence trail might be gone by then. It was time to take back control.

The bank would be closed, so she headed to their apartment. Blake might even be home. When she entered, his was there with his back to her.

"Hey," she said.

He spun around, and his eyes widened. "I didn't expect you home so soon."

She had called to tell him about Danita and to say she wasn't sure when she would make it home, but he hadn't answered the call. It was possible he had been too busy to respond.

"I called you."

He patted his pocket. "Shit. I turned my phone to silent when I was meeting with someone. I'm sorry. What did you need to tell me?"

She repeated what happened to Danita, though if he hadn't seen her message, why did he think she was late arriving home? Most likely, he'd lost track of time.

"Danita regained consciousness and told me something very

interesting."

"What was it?"

Greer lifted her chin. "I know where the Changeling is."

"Seriously?" He averted his gaze as if her news disturbed him.

"Is something wrong?" She stepped closer. Blake was sending out some strange signals, but she couldn't be sure what they meant.

"No. I want to find this Changeling as much as you do."

"Good. Let's change. We need to look for this wolf."

He held up his hands. "Now?"

"Yes now. I know where his new campsite is. Between Danita and Griffin, I'm pretty sure I can find it."

"For real?"

That wasn't the response she expected. What the hell was going on? "Yes, for real. This creep took Danita there, attacked her, and then left her for dead. If she hadn't been able to call Griffin to come get her, she would have died."

Blake glanced to the side. "Okay. Calm down. I'll make you some peach tea. Go change, and then we can do our search."

Blake was acting strange. "I don't need any tea."

"Well, I do. It will help me focus."

She'd never even seen him drink tea, though with everything that had happened recently, she wasn't surprised that Blake might be coming unglued. First Kaleena was arrested, and then Danita was attacked. "Fine. I'll change."

The teabag box was on the counter just where she'd left it yesterday, which probably made him think of brewing some.

When he smiled, the familiar lustful rush of hormones failed to fill her. Then Greer's thoughts cleared, and she stiffened. This wasn't Blake, but rather the Changeling. Holy shit.

Not having a plan, Greer rushed into the bedroom, closed the door, and pressed her back against it. Shit. She pulled out her phone to text Blake. Oh, no. If this man looked like Blake then clearly he'd been in contact with her mate. The big question was had he harmed him? Knowing the werewolf would become suspicious if she took too longer, she texted Blake. Before she had the chance to finish, the man pushed open the door. "Are you okay? You seem a bit off."

She gave him her best smile. "No. I'm still thinking about Danita."

"Your tea is ready."

"Thanks. I'll be ready in a second."

He ducked out. Greer quickly changed. Her plan was to get him outside, shift, and then fly his sorry werewolf ass to the police station where she would deposit him on the front steps.

With a plan in place, she returned to the kitchen, where the Changeling was dipping the tea bag in the hot water.

"Drink this while I change."

Whatever. As soon as the doppelganger went into bedroom, she took a few sips, relaxing for just a moment. When she'd almost finished, she pulled out her phone to complete her text to Blake, but her eyes refused to focus. What the hell? Before she could even send what she had or call for help, the werewolf returned, dressed in one of Blake's red and blue plaid shirt.

"Ready?" he asked, his face now a blur.

She grabbed hold of the counter. "Blake, I'm feeling a little funny." That was the truth. "I think I'll rest first."

Before she could reach the bedroom, Greer lost consciousness.

WHEN BLAKE FINALLY opened his eyes, he couldn't figure out why he was on the floor of his office, staring at the legs of his desk. His mouth was sand dry, and his vision was a bit blurry. Aw, hell. Had he fainted? The last thing he remembered was talking with Belinda, his secretary. They were looking at something on his computer while he was drinking the cup of coffee she'd brought him.

Then what happened? Crap. It was as if someone had erased his memory. Belinda probably came and left, and then he'd passed out.

Pushing up to a seated position, he glanced around. How long had he been unconscious? The lights outside his office were out. Disgusted that he'd collapsed without remembering anything, he managed to stand. Thankfully, the dizziness that assaulted him quickly dissipated. Whatever had happened, his dragon had mostly healed him, albeit slowly.

Only because this was déjà vu all over again from when he'd been taken over by that dark entity did he check to see if he had any injuries. He lifted his shirt and looked. No dark marks were there, making him conclude no other dark entity had entered the realm.

His coffee cup was still on his desk. When he picked it up, it smelled kind of funny. Oh, shit, had he been drugged? By Belinda? Just as he was about to call her to find out what she knew, he checked his watch and was stunned to find it was past six. Crap.

By now, Greer would have been home for a while and probably had called to see when he was returning.

He checked his phone. Sure enough, there were two messages. He listened to them, stunned to learn that Danita had been attacked by a wolf. Greer was helping to heal her and wasn't sure when she would get home. The second message was also from Greer. She told him that Danita would be okay, and that the wolf had red eyes. She was on her way home now and hoped they could search for this evil being tonight.

What the hell was going on here? The only logical explanation was the Changeling was involved in this mess. Damn it.

Blake looked around his office to make sure nothing obvious had been stolen, but everything seemed undisturbed. He quickly checked his laptop for an obvious breach but found none either.

Needing to make sure Greer was safe, he grabbed his laptop and headed out the building's back door—a door that required his security code to unlock.

Once upstairs in his apartment, he was surprised he didn't sense her. "Greer, honey, are you here?"

When she didn't answer, his pulse soared. The most likely explanation was that either Kaleena was having issues again or Danita still needed her. If she'd been with Danita, the werewolf wouldn't have gotten to her.

Blake first called Greer, but her cell went to voicemail. Thankfully, she had insisted that Blake have everyone's number programmed into his cell just in case he needed to contact someone. Everyone had his in case his skills were needed.

Next, he called Kaleena, since he didn't know how to get a hold of Danita.

"Hello?"

"Kaleena, it's Blake. Is Greer there by any chance?"

"No."

"Have you seen her since we saw you at the police station?" His pulse beat hard.

"No, but I heard that Danita had been injured, and that Griffin needed Greer's healing abilities for her."

"She left me a voicemail to that effect. Thanks." Apparently, Guardians shared everything. "I'll call Griffin and see what he can tell me."

Griffin answered on the first ring. "Blake. What's up?"

"I'm looking for Greer. Is she with you?"

"No, she left over an hour ago. Why?"

"I thought she'd be home by now. Greer left a message saying that Danita needed her gift of healing."

"Sadly, yes. Some red-eyed werewolf attacked Danita. Even though she had lost a lot of blood, she managed to call me and tell me where she was. When I got to the forest, the werewolf was nowhere to be found. I took Danita back to the safe house and immediately asked Greer for help."

"How is Danita now?"

"Good, thanks to Greer. Oh, crap. If my sister is not with you, I wouldn't be surprised if she went out there to look for that monster herself."

Shit. Shit. Shit. "Where is this place?" Griffin gave him the directions. "Thanks."

"If I didn't need to stay with Danita, I'd come with you."

"I can handle a wolf. Trust me."

Every cell in his body went haywire. Only now did it occur to him that when Belinda was in his office, she was acting a bit strange. He'd asked her a few questions about one of the accounts, and she said she didn't remember the details—something that never happened.

Right now, Blake needed to find his mate. When he went to look for his car keys, which he always left on the counter in a bowl, they were gone. Then a wisp of gray essence mixed with Greer's golden aura floated by. Fuck. This was not good. In fact, it was totally bad. The Changeling had been here.

Her purse was tossed on the sofa, causing his blood pressure to skyrocket. On the off-chance Blake was wrong about seeing the Changeling's trail, he ran into the bedroom, hoping to see Greer asleep on the bed. Her work clothes were strewn across the chair, but she wasn't there. More fear spiked through him.

Almost in full-blown panic mode now, he ran back to the living room and searched Greer's purse for her keys. When he found them, he sighed a breath of relief. Not that he couldn't fly to the forest, but once there, walking the seemingly endless miles to the middle of the woodland on foot would be slow going.

Blake debated calling Finn to ask for his help because he was a wolf, but what if Kaleena needed her mate? After some debate, Blake decided to find Greer on his own.

As fast as he could, he drove through town, but to his dismay all of the stoplights seemed to have it in for him. It took forever to be free of traffic. While Greer's essence trail had been in the apartment, it had disappeared as soon as he went downstairs to the parking lot in back—and so had the gray essence trail that had mingled with her golden one.

Poor Greer. This guy had to be stopped. Every killer, thief, and miscreant could claim that some Changeling had touched him and then committed a crime in his name. The irony of it wasn't lost on

Blake since that was exactly what had happened to him with Mange.

His mind refused to stop spinning about how to approach this monster—or rather whether to kill him out right. The fact this freak had possibly harmed his mate meant all bets were off.

Frustration drove him harder. Once he made it to the forest, his thoughts turned a bit more rational. Killing the Changeling might cause issues for Greer and her family, and he wouldn't do that to her. Knocking the guy unconscious however was definitely in the cards. Unfortunately, Finn hadn't really known the limits of the Changeling's magical powers. Could this guy put a spell on him, like, freeze him in time? Greer had told him how some dark lighter had done that to Thane. Bottom line was that Blake had to be cautious.

Possibly because it was past sunset that Blake almost missed spotting his black car off to the side of the road. With no other vehicles close by, he pulled onto the shoulder, cut the engine, and jumped out.

As soon as he headed down the trail, he was able to pick up both essence trails, even though they were faint. At least he was in the right spot. His slight joy was short lived when he imagined what that red-eyed werewolf was doing to her. He fisted his hands, trying to calm down enough to remain cautious—a very difficult chore indeed.

A SHARP PAIN stabbed the back of Greer's head, her spine, and her hip, jarring her out of her stupor. The motherfucker had drugged her. From the fact she was on cold, hard ground meant he'd somehow managed to take her into the forest.

Crickets were making a racket, and leaves were crunching. The Changeling was close. Greer opened her eyes and saw Blake's doppelganger. She might have thought it was Blake, except there were no waves of desire coursing through her body. It didn't matter she was injured. She would have sensed the sexual draw between them. Greer pushed up on her elbows but fell back down.

He rushed over. "Easy now. You're okay." He sounded so much like her Blake and even acted really concerned. Even though this wasn't her mate, she wouldn't let on that she knew.

"What happened?" she asked.

"You tell me," he said.

"I must have passed out. Healing Danita took a lot out of me, I guess." Even Greer was impressed with her improvised reasoning. "But why am I here?"

"That Changeling took you here."

This man was a terrible liar, but she shuttered her disbelief. What she needed to know was what had caused her to pass out? Shit. The tea! He must have spiked it with something. Jerk. "How did you find me?"

Let him answer that question, Mr. Changeling man.

Chapter Seventeen

G RUNTS AND SHOUTS, together with the impact of fists meeting flesh, roused Greer again. She opened her eyes and had to blink. Crap. She didn't remember passing out again. That tea must have had a really strong sedative in it or else her dragon would have healed her already.

Greer blinked again. Yup. She was seeing double. Now there were two Blakes, both dressed in the identical long sleeve black shirt and hiking pants. What happened to the man who had hovered over her a moment ago—the one wearing flannel?

When one of the men grunted, her mind somewhat cleared. The real Blake had come to save her, but she couldn't figure out which one was her mate. With the men moving around so much, she couldn't identify where the sexual draw was coming from. At least she was certain there weren't two Changelings fighting. One for sure was her mate.

The man on the left landed a blow to the jaw of the man on the right, causing him to drop to one knee. Ouch. If only she knew whether to cry out or cheer. She waited for the Changeling to turn into a wolf or for Blake to transform his hands into fire-throwing claws, but so far that hadn't happened. She could understand her mate not shifting into a dragon since he'd have no room to maneuver, but why not transform his hands? That would stop the Changeling from attacking.

The unidentified man on the ground rose to his feet and raised his arm as if to shoot fire, only his arm didn't become a dragon's claw. Was this Blake who had his powers dampened by the

Changeling, or was it the Changeling himself? And why was everything so fuzzy?

The first man did some kind of roundhouse kick, knocking the other man to the ground. The injured man slowly rose to his feet. Her heart pounded at the beating. *Please don't let that be my mate.*

The two men circled each other, swung, staggered, and punched again. If the Changeling managed to defeat Blake, what would she do?

What was she talking about? She was a Guardian. She'd burn his ass, assuming she could tell the last man standing was Blake. Surely, when she kissed him, she'd know for sure, though was she willing to kiss a Changeling and chance something really bad might happen?

Stop this madness. I'd know. It wouldn't take a kiss. These drugs were messing with her mind.

Determined to help, Greer rose to her feet and immediately dropped down to her knees.

Come on and heal me, she demanded of her dragon.

I'm trying. The drug he gave you is still doing some serious damage to my abilities.

Can I shoot fire out of my arm at least? she asked.

I don't know. We need to get out of here though.

Are you kidding me? What about Blake? She couldn't leave him.

He can take care of himself, her animal shot back.

Never!

It was possible Blake was trying to fight fairly because she was there. If he knew she was safe, he might change his tactics.

You need to leave, her dragon urged.

If she stayed, she probably wouldn't be of much use to Blake anyway, but she could never abandon her mate. Using all of her willpower, Greer rose to her unsteady feet. Thankfully, neither man seemed to notice that she'd roused and was more or less standing. The dense foliage in this area would prevent her from shifting though.

One of the men looked over at her and smiled. Her heart

throbbed. That had to be Blake. As if her being awake gave him the added boost, he raised his arms again. This time they changed into claws, and the Changeling's eyes widened. He immediately transformed into a wolf and darted into the woods.

Greer wanted to shout out to Blake to burn the guy's ass, or at the very least go after him, but on foot, Blake wouldn't be able to catch him.

Blake lowered his arms and rushed over to her. "Are you okay?"

Her head swam as the surge of poison, confusion, and trauma all collided. "Yes. No. That Changeling drugged me." She held up her hands. "I just need…" What did she need? "Time."

"Time? Are you sure you're okay?"

It was all too much to take in. Maybe Greer had never fully dealt with having been drugged and kidnapped by that dark entity who looked like Blake. Now, that same man was standing in front of her. She'd seen the other man transform into a wolf and could tell by the attraction between them that this was her mate. Any logical person would throw herself into his arms, but the drugs, as well as her past collided, causing a maelstrom of confusion. "I have to go," she said, her voice way too high.

Before she said or did anything she'd regret, she turned and raced down the path. If she didn't get her head on straight, no telling what might happen.

"Greer! Wait!" Blake called.

As much as she wanted to stop, she couldn't afford to—both for her sake and for his. In truth, she expected him to run after her, but he must have seen the panic in her eyes and decided to give her what she'd asked for—some time to come to grips with what had occurred. Fighting the nausea and dizzying effect of the drug, she did her best to make it down the path without tripping.

It felt like hours before she came to the road. Relief swamped her when she saw that her car was parked next to Blake's. Considering her weak muscles, she would be better off flying, but she was uncertain where to go. If she returned to the condo, the Changeling might find her.

Her first instinct was to call her sister, Nessa—calm, level headed Nessa—instead of Tory who would tell her to rush back to Blake. That advice might seem sound, but it didn't sit well with her at the moment.

So, Nessa it was. Thankfully, Greer had put her phone in her pocket right before she'd entered the apartment. She called her sister, hoping she'd answer.

"Greer, hey," Nessa said.

"I'm in trouble."

"What happened?" Nessa asked, straight to the point.

As briefly as she could, Greer explained about how after treating Danita she came home to find a man who she thought was Blake at first—only it was the Changeling.

"Oh, shit. You couldn't tell it wasn't your mate?"

Now Greer felt stupid. "I knew something was off, but I was a little weak from treating Danita to think much of it. He said a few odd things, and only then did I realize what he was. Long story short, he insisted I drink some peach tea to help calm me. At the time, I didn't know it was drugged. Before I could call Blake or Anderson, I passed out. Somehow, I ended up in the woods."

"That's horrifying. How did you escape?"

She detailed how Blake—the real one—came and fought off the Changeling. "He's okay, but I can't deal with him now. I know I hurt him when I said I needed space, but it's like the world is closing in on me. I've never felt like this before in my life. I'm always in control."

"I know just the person to help you."

"Who?"

BLAKE WAS STUNNED by what just happened. As much as he wanted to run after Greer and comfort her, the way her eyes were darting back and forth and her hands shaking, she needed some personal space. Fire ignited his gut just knowing the Changeling had done something to mess with her head this much. Being this helpless wasn't an emotion he was used to. Blake paced, trying to decide his next move. "Fuck."

As much as he wanted to race down the path and catch up with her, Blake walked back to her car instead, trying to figure out how to help her.

By the time he reached the road, Greer's essence trail had faded considerable. Both cars were parked next to each other, implying she was either hiding somewhere or she'd flown away. He looked down the road and spotted wisps of her golden aura in the direction away from town. He hadn't expected that. Why would she go that way? Shit.

Blake was more confused than ever. Greer probably believed the Changeling might try to come after her again. Since the wolf had escaped, it was a logical conclusion.

He patted his pockets. Crap. He had her car keys, and he bet the Changeling still had the keys to Blake's car.

Blake glanced at his hand. Warm blood was dripping across his palm. When he unrolled the sleeves of his now ripped shirt, he found the source. The Changeling must have cut him with his sharpened claws. He should have healed by now, but Blake was still feeling the effects from the drugs in his system. Maybe now wasn't the best time to try to talk some sense into Greer since he wasn't of sound mind yet himself. He certainly didn't want to upset her any more than she already was.

After he cleaned up the cut the best he could, he slid into Greer's car and stabbed the key in the ignition. Griffin! He'd probably know where Greer might have gone. Being the eldest, Greer's brother seemed to have his pulse on everything that went on in his family.

Blake called him, and he answered immediately. "Blake? You find the son of a bitch?"

"Yes, but he got away."

"Oh, shit. How's Greer? Did you find her?"

"Yes." He explained how he'd found her on the ground. "Even after she woke up, she was disoriented. The Changeling had drugged her too. Greer then said that she couldn't deal being with me for the moment. Something about needing some space."

"If Greer had been drugged, it might have brought back all of those memories of her previous capture—you know, the one that involved you."

"You're probably right."

"Where are you now?" Griffin asked.

"At the entrance to the path leading to the Changeling's campsite."

"I have an idea. It'll be faster to tell you what I'm thinking if I come to you. Let me make a few phone calls. I'll see you in a few."

"Sure." If Griffin thought it best to come to him, so be it.

GREER WASN'T EXPECTING Nessa to suggest that Greer speak with Fay Forester, but the fairy had helped several members of her family in the past. It certainly couldn't hurt to find out what she had to say.

It had been a long time since Greer had visited the eternal flame, but apparently that was where Fay lived. In need of some serious help in figuring out how to deal with what she'd been through, Greer rejoiced when she was able to shift and take off.

To make sure she was back to normal, she opened her mouth to shoot out flames, but nothing happened. Damn. If she ever got close to that Changeling again, she'd kill him herself. No question about it.

She flew over the parkway close to the ground until she was out from under the dense foliage. Thankfully, few cars were on the road at that hour. The only positive of having to fly halfway across the realm was that the longer she was in her dragon form, the better chance her body had to heal.

Partway into her journey, guilt assaulted her at her decision to leave Blake. Logically, it had been selfish of her to run away, but emotionally, she needed to give them some separation. Greer just hoped Blake wouldn't be too upset that she'd left him to make his own way home. Yes, he'd worry about her, but he was better off not having to deal with her in her stressed mental state.

Or was she rationalizing her behavior again? Damned if she knew.

Keeping an eye on where she was going, she'd traveled about an hour before spotting the line of trees that signaled the beginning of the forest where the eternal flame was located. Greer landed. The dense foliage required her to go the rest of the way on foot. Because this was a bit of a tourist attraction, there was thankfully a sign pointing to the path that led to her destination.

The flat wide path allowed her to move quickly. To her delight, her energy had returned almost completely. Thank goodness her dragon had succeeded in removing the poison from her system.

When the path dead-ended, had it not been for the light from the eternal flame, she would have been convinced she had taken a wrong turn. The whole setup was a lot more unassuming than she remembered the first time she came here. Then again, that was over eighty years ago.

Noisy animals indicated some evidence of life. The absence of any fairies concerned her though. At Birk's wedding, Fay had shown up—first as a swarm of what looked like fireflies and then as a beautiful blonde woman.

Greer waited to be approached. And she kept waiting. Apparently, Fay had *office hours*. It was possible she only showed up during the day. Well, that sucked.

"Hello?" Greer called out.

When no one answered, she stepped over to the flames and peered into the light. She loved the flickering and the heat. Fire always soothed her. If she looked long enough, she might even figure out the answer to her own problems. She not only had concerns about what the Changeling incident would do to her relationship with Blake, she was also concerned with what the werewolf would do next.

Darn it. She should probably just fly back home and confront the issue by telling Blake how wrong she'd been to leave.

Greer spun around to head back out of the forest to do just that. She'd taken less than three steps when a woman stepped out of the woods, startling her.

"Hello," said the stranger.

This wasn't Fay, but rather a short woman with light brown hair. "Hi, I'm looking for Fay Forrester."

"She's not available. I'm her sister, Meena."

Greer had no idea Fay had siblings. "I'm Greer—"

"Caspian. Yes, I know."

"How did you know that?" she shot back with a bit too much edge to her voice.

Meena chuckled. "Let's have a seat over here on the rock where we can chat. I hear there's been a stranger in our midst."

Her knowledge of the evil stranger kind of freaked Greer out, yet it comforted her at the same time to know this woman had special talents. "Has he been here?"

She tapped the area on the rock next to her. "No."

Greer blew out a breath. This was overwhelming. The white entity, Angelique, seemed to have special powers. The fact she came from a different realm made it understandable. Some white lighters were psychic. Was Meena?

"I see."

"Tell me what brings you here," Meena said.

"You don't know?" Hadn't she just said she knew there was a stranger in their midst? Okay, more proof that Greer was losing it. If nothing else, she was always the epitome of poise and calm. Now she was not. "I'm sorry. That was uncalled for."

"Don't worry about it. I sense you've been through a lot. And I mean a lot. I want you to tell me in your own words what's going on," Meena said.

Greer didn't know where to begin. Her entire world had collapsed when that dark lighter had stabbed her in the neck. Finding her mate had changed her life for the good, but it had thrown her ability to make clear decisions off kilter. "It all started when a dark lighter from a different realm took over the body of my mate." She explained about being abducted and how she'd found Blake.

"Did you believe he was your mate at first? I mean you wouldn't have known he'd been taken over by a dark entity."

"Not until the dark entity left his body."

"Then what happened?"

"A Changeling from Earth arrived." Greer explained about his abilities and how when she arrived home to their apartment this evening, a man who looked like Blake had drugged her tea and then kidnapped her.

"How terrible."

"It was. When I awoke in the woods and saw Blake's doppelganger, I was scared. I must have passed out again, because when I woke up again, I found two men—both of who looked like Blake—fighting each other."

"How confusing! You must be traumatized."

"I am." It was wonderful to have someone to talk to who seemed to understand.

"Go on."

Greer was ashamed to tell her. "After my mate chased off the madman, I left. I have no defense for my actions. I was so confused that I told him I needed my space."

"I see." Meena clasped her hand. "You did the right thing in coming here."

"Do you really think so?"

"I know so."

Tears leaked out of her eyes—tears of joy. "Thank you. What should I do now? Head back to town and find him?"

Meena smiled. "I have just the thing. There is a cabin I've set up just for you about a half mile or so down that path."

Birk had told her about this cabin and had said the white wooden home was adorable and perfect. "You don't think I should explain to Blake why I just up and left?"

"After you rest, you'll have plenty of time to tell him everything. And do try the tub. A good soak can do wonders for your clarity of mind."

She was more confused than ever. "You didn't know I was coming here, so how did you know to prepare this cabin? Or did Nessa call you?"

"No one called me." Meena laughed. "I just knew." She gave Greer's hand a squeeze and then let go. "By tomorrow morning, all of your worries—or rather most of them—will be gone."

Now she was talking crazy, but the idea of a relaxing night to think would be so welcome. "Is there any way that Changeling can find me?"

"The fairies will make certain no one harms you."

"That sounds wonderful." Greer pointed to the most prominent path. "I just go down that path for half a mile and I'll find it?"

Meena smiled and then stood. "It would be better if you follow me."

Before Greer could tell her guide that she could find it on her own, Meena changed into these tiny points of light. In a V-shaped pattern, she flew down the path, and Greer trailed after her.

As Greer walked down the tree covered path, her thoughts shot back to Blake, wishing he was with her instead of the terrible guilt that had assaulted her earlier.

Greer must not have been paying attention, because it was as if a cabin appeared out of thin air. Only it wasn't the white wooden cabin with the green shutters that her brother and his mate had described. This was a rather upscale cabin with lots of windows. While there wasn't a front porch, the tall soaring sides created from some kind of sleek stone she'd never seen before, made up for it. "Wow."

When she turned to thank Meena, every bit of light was gone. All that was left was a quick shot of cold air that blew past her. Now that was almost creepy.

"Meena?"

Greer waited for a moment, and when she didn't appear, she hurried up the path to the front of the house. The front door was unlocked, so Greer stepped inside. When she flicked on the light, her heart pounded at the amazing interior. Everything was classy and upscale, not at all what she expected from a cabin in the woods. Blake would love this place too. She should call him and invite him to join her. Unfortunately, when she pulled out her phone, it indicated there was no service. "Great."

Given the late hour, Greer would stay here tonight and return home tomorrow to the man she loved.

Chapter Eighteen

A S SOON AS Griffin landed, he shifted and then shook Blake's hand. "I spoke with Nessa. She said she heard from Greer."

He blew out a breath. "Does she know where she is?"

"Nessa suggested that Greer speak with Fay Forrester."

"Who is she? I've never heard of her."

"She's a fairy, but I can't tell you what her powers are exactly. All I know is that both Nessa and Birk have spoken at length with her. Both said she *knew* things. Their word, not mine."

"Nessa said Greer was rather confused, and that she sounded exhausted too. She sent her to Fay in hopes she would help her get things straightened out with whatever caused her to run. Also, Nessa said there was a cabin in the woods, and she is hoping Fay might put Greer up there to relax and calm down."

"Good to know, but why go to a fairy?" Hell, he didn't even know they existed. Then again, he'd never heard of Changelings before either. He really needed to get out more.

"Fay might be able to tell her how to defeat this guy, or how to deal with her feelings about both of her abductions. It's hard to say which."

That made sense. "Where is this Fay woman now? I know it's late, but do you think she'll be around?"

Griffin shrugged. "If that is where Greer is, you should go. I would suggest you wait a bit before running after her to give her some time to come to grips with things."

"She's already had a half hour head start."

Griffin wrapped an arm around his shoulder. "I can't say I'm an expert with women, but I know my sister. Give her another hour and then head out after her. It wouldn't be a bad idea to go home and shower either."

He did look a mess. He also probably smelled. "I don't want her to be alone. What if she can't find this Fay woman?"

"Okay, you can skip the shower, but don't rush out right away."

"I'll take your advice. You never said where I could find this fairy chick."

"She's at the eternal flame."

"The one that's in the middle of the realm?"

"The one and only. It's where Fay lives—or should I say where she flits about. Just so you know, Fay will probably be in her lightning bug form."

Okay, this was getting crazier by the minute. "Maybe this isn't such a good idea."

"You don't have any hope of finding Greer if you don't go through Fay. In my heart, I believe my sister needs you."

"Right. Just not immediately."

Griffin smiled. "Exactly. I'd go with you, but I need to get back to make sure Danita is okay. Being attacked by that wolf really set her back."

He wouldn't think of taking anyone away from a person in need. "Thanks for everything."

"Let me know how it works out." Griffin gave him general directions on how to find the flame. Blake had been once years ago, but he appreciated the repeated information.

Griffin took off and Blake headed back down the trail in search of the small stream he'd seen. While he couldn't completely clean up, he didn't want to scare Greer with smeared blood, though by the time he flew to the center of Tarradon, his dragon would have healed any major cuts and scrapes.

Once clean, he trotted back to the area where he'd fought with the Changeling. When the man shifted, his clothes ripped apart. That meant Blake's car keys would be somewhere on the ground.

While it was dark, his excellent eyesight enabled him to find them close to the path. Dropping them in his pocket, he took off again, ready to search for Greer. Griffin had assured him it wouldn't be too hard to find the flame. After all, it was Tarradon's national treasure.

All during his long flight, he kept spotting bits and pieces of Greer's light trail, which gave him comfort that he was headed in the right direction. At the forest entrance, her essence turned rather wispy, indicating she'd passed this way a while ago. He hoped he'd given her enough time to calm down, though after all she'd been through, ninety minutes might not be enough.

Blake landed at the trailhead and then shifted. To his delight, there was a wooden sign that pointed to the eternal flame trailhead. Now that he was near her, Blake couldn't wait any longer to hold Greer in his arms and tell her all would be okay. He jogged down the path, searching for more of her essence. He spotted it at random intervals, but he had no idea why it was appearing and then fading. It was almost as if this place was trying to hide her—something that was possible considering Griffin claimed this fairy was magical.

When he came to the end of the path, he was surprised it wasn't guarded.

"Greer?" he called out, though he didn't expect her to hear him. If she had been close, he would have sensed her presence.

He paced the small space, trying to figure out his next move. Blake must have been there a good ten minutes when a man stepped from behind a tree and startled him. He hadn't even known anyone was near, which was not like him.

"Welcome," the stranger said. "I'm Kenton Forrester, Fay's brother. Are you looking for Greer?"

Blake had called out her name. "Yes. Have you seen her?"

"Not personally, but my sister, Meena, told me that Greer is staying in our cabin."

Griffin told him about the cabin too. "That's great. Where is this place? I need to see her."

"I want to show you something first."

Not that Blake didn't believe this guy was on the up and up, especially since he knew about Greer, but Blake was capable of finding his mate on his own. "That's okay. If you point me in the right direction, I'm sure I can find her."

Kenton held up his hand. "You don't trust me. I get it. Greer is your mate, and you want to protect her."

Alarms were going off in his head. "Precisely."

"Whether you like it or not, you need me to reach her. I will show you where she is, but first, come see this," he demanded, even though his tone held nothing but humor. Kenton walked to the other side of the eternal flame to a small cement fountain.

Given this guy wasn't any kind of shifter, Blake could take him if need be even though he wasn't any diminutive fairy who would fly away, that was for sure. When Blake stepped next to Kenton, the long-haired man closed his eyes and held his hands over the water. He mumbled something in a language Blake had never heard before. When he looked down at the surface of the water, his muscles froze. In it was the reflection of Greer speaking to a small woman with similar colored brown hair to Kenton's.

"Thank you. What should I do now?" That was Greer speaking to this woman. It was as if this guy had recorded their conversation and was playing it somehow in the water. When Blake looked around however, he didn't spot any cameras.

"That's my sister Meena," Kenton said. "Watch."

Meena smiled. *"I have just the thing. There is a cabin I've set up just for you about a half mile or so down that path."*

"You don't think I should return to town and explain to Blake why I just up and left?"

Blake's heart pounded. He'd been wondering if she would feel bad for basically running away. Now he knew the answer.

"After you rest, you'll have plenty of time to tell him everything. And do try the tub. A good soak can do wonders for your clarity of mind."

"You couldn't have known I was coming here. Did Nessa call you or

something"?

"No one called me." Meena laughed. *"I just knew."* She clasped Greer's hand. *"By tomorrow morning, all of your worries—or rather most of them—will be gone."*

"Is there any way that Changeling can find me?"

"The fairies will make certain no one harms you."

"That sounds wonderful." Greer pointed to the most prominent path. *"I just go down that path for half a mile and I'll find it?"*

"Yes. Follow me."

The image disappeared and returned to being an ordinary looking pool of water. Blake spun around to face Kenton. "What just happened?"

"What do you mean? I wanted to show you that I mean you no harm, and I thought this would be the proof you needed."

Kenton was right. Blake had needed proof. This man had some serious powers. Even a Changeling couldn't have pulled that off. "Okay. I'm sorry I jumped down your throat. I'm just so worried about Greer."

Kenton nodded. "No problem. Come with me."

"You don't have to walk with me. Just tell me where the cabin is."

"I'm afraid you can only find it if one of us guides you there."

"Are you going to turn into a firefly now and lead the way?" Blake honestly had no idea what a male fairy was capable of.

Kenton laughed. "I'm not a fairy. I'm a fey. Trust me, there is a big difference. My mother is a fairy, and my dad is a fey. Meena, Fay, and Tally are fairies, while Beven and I are fey. We don't turn into light like our sisters do."

"Good to know."

"Come on."

As nice as this guy was, Blake was willing to let him lead but that was all. Even though Blake kept looking for this cabin, nothing resembled any kind of structure. "Are you sure you know where it is?"

"I do. In fact, we are here," Kenton said.

"Where?" Blake had excellent eyesight, especially in the dark, but nothing was there. He was certain of it.

"Right there." The moment this fey pointed to the woods, a house appeared out of thin air.

"Holy shit. How did you do that?"

"Ah, I see I've finally impressed you. Now go see your mate."

Blake turned around to thank him, but Kenton had disappeared. "Thank you," Blake called to the air.

He must be losing his mind. Without waiting any longer, he raced up the short path to the rather modern looking cabin. As soon as he lifted his hand to knock, waves of sexual excitement coursed through him. Yes! Greer was definitely here!

GREER LEANED HER head back against the tub, the soap bubbles covering most of her body. The heat and the quiet helped calm her racing mind. If it hadn't been for Meena's promise that all would be well, Greer probably would have flown back to town. She had freaked out Blake and hurt his feelings, but she couldn't handle dealing with even one more thing at that moment. First, she'd take a soak and then get a solid night's sleep. Tomorrow morning, she'd return to town to repair the damage she'd caused to their relationship.

If she had been in her right mind, she would have done a better job explaining things to him. Never having had a panic attack before meant she hadn't been able to express herself clearly.

At the time, she feared that the Changeling might return and battle with Blake again in order to get to her. Or wasn't that the real reason? Hell if she knew.

She shook her head at how stupid she'd been from the moment she entered the apartment. She should have noticed the man was an impostor right from the start. Then there was the tea. How did he know she loved peach tea? It could have been Blake's. She didn't want to think he'd been watching her for a while.

Oh crap. She'd ordered peach tea at Angelique's coffee shop. It was possible he'd been a waitress there or another customer. She shivered at that creepy thought.

Greer needed to stop thinking about what she'd done wrong and focus on what she would do the next time she saw Blake. A small smile crept up her face. She knew the first thing she'd do. She'd tempt him and tease him until he forgave her. After they had an amazing lovemaking session, she'd calmly explain her faulty reasoning for leaving. He'd forgive her—or so she hoped.

The water in the tub had turned a bit tepid, so she drained a bit of it while turning on the hot water. Just as it reached the perfect temperature, something blocked the lamplight streaming in from the bedroom. She looked up.

"Blake?" Or was it the Changeling? Her body said it was her mate, but maybe she wasn't capable of knowing the difference. "Is that really you?"

Blake grinned and moved closer, forcing Greer to cross her hands over her breasts. It didn't matter she was covered by the bubbles or that lust was shooting through her.

Blake smiled. "Yes, Greer. It's me. Really."

Greer lifted her chin. "Prove it." A twinkle shot to his eyes. He unsnapped his jeans and had his pants halfway pulled down when she grinned. Only Blake would do that. "Okay, okay. Tell me this, Mr. Hard Body, where did we first meet?"

It was stupid to question him when her pussy was lighting up like the midday sun, but her illogical brain demanded she ask. Greer wasn't sure she'd survive if this Changeling fooled her again. That newcomer from Earth wouldn't know anything about the inauspicious start to their relationship, so this was a good test.

Blake kicked off his boots and then dragged off his pants, along with his briefs.

"I came into the jewelry store to buy a ring. Before I could, this dark entity you called Mange inhabited my body, making me stab you in the neck with a tranquilizer." His brows rose, as if he was waiting for her to give him the all clear.

She leaned her head against the tub's rim. "I knew it was you. I just wanted to see you naked."

"Uh huh."

She lowered her hands and planted her elbows on the edge. "I'm sorry I left in a huff."

"You don't need to explain. I understand. You were over-whelmed." He held up his palms. "I spoke with Griffin, and he assured me you were merely having something like a panic attack, and it wasn't anything I had done."

"That's totally what happened. I think it was partially that I've never dealt with the first kidnapping that caused the meltdown. Then when I feared the Changeling might best you, my brain cells disconnected."

He tossed off his shirt. "You have nothing to worry about. I'm good. If you don't mind, I need to get clean from all that rolling around in the dirt and frenlen needles. I don't want to mess up your bath, so I'll just step in the shower."

"I'll help you wash." Being around Blake helped settled her soul and her heart.

She stood, and his eyes turned that gorgeous teal, causing her libido to catch on fire. Blake approached. He held out his hand and helped her out of the tub.

"You are a sight for sore eyes," he said. "When I saw you lying on the ground like that, I was scared shitless that the Changeling had harmed you."

"Other than drugging me with the peach tea, he didn't hurt me." Greer grabbed a towel and wrapped it around her body.

"Same here, only it was with coffee." He explained how the Changeling must have pretended to be his secretary. "She offered me a drink, and I didn't think anything of it. Only after I thought about it did I suspect something wasn't right, I had asked Belinda a few questions that she should have known the answers to. By that time though, I had become dizzy. Next thing I remember, I woke up sprawled out on the floor and two hours had passed."

Greer gritted her teeth. "I want to kill the bastard."

Blake dragged a hand down her shoulder, his touch calming her. "How about we worry about him later? I have a lot of other things on my mind besides an insidiously terrible werewolf." Blake ran his gaze down her body, heating up her interior scales.

"Is that so? And what would those things be?" she asked as innocently as possible.

Chapter Nineteen

"**F**OR STARTERS, THIS." Blake drew her close and kissed her. Wow. No doubt about it, this was most definitely her Blake Masters. No one kissed like he did. How she hadn't been able to tell him and the Changeling apart during the fight still confused her, but it didn't matter now. They were here together, and she planned to do whatever it took to keep it that way.

Even though she was getting him all wet, Blake didn't seem to mind. He finally broke the kiss. "If I don't stop, I'll be dragging you to bed, and I know I smell."

"You do." She was only teasing him, but it did her soul wonders to relax around him. She patted him on the butt. "Let's hop in the shower. I promised I'd help you."

Blake stepped in and turned on the water. Greer dropped her towel from around her body and joined him.

His eyes widened. "How am I supposed to concentrate with you all naked?"

"You are funny, but who says you have to concentrate? That's why I'm here. To help you get clean."

Greer picked up the soap, wet it, and then dragged it down his chest. He clasped her wrist. "Maybe I should do that."

"Because I'll distract you too much?" She'd forgotten how wonderful flirting could be.

"Yes."

She lifted her chin. "Okay. I'll rinse and get out of your way then." The only problem with taking a bath was that afterward she needed to wash off the soapy water.

Greer dunked under the powerful stream, did a superficial cleaning, and stepped out of the shower onto the bathmat.

"I'll be quick." Blake scrubbed his arms and legs. Once he finished with his face, he washed his hair and then rinsed.

After turning off the shower. When he stepped on the mat, Greer was there with a towel. She patted his chest, enjoying how his black scales pulsed against his sand colored ones, and his eyes shimmered that pretty teal.

The fact she'd walked away from him this evening still boggled her mind. What had she been thinking pushing him away like that? Now wasn't the right time to think about it though. As Blake said, they had other things on their minds—like making love. More than anything, Greer wanted to make their mating official.

When she finished dragging the towel down his chest, she took hold of his cock.

"You're asking for trouble," Blake said with a grin.

"I like trouble."

"Is that so? Let's see how much trouble we can get into then."

Greer laughed for the first time in what seemed like days. "You're on."

He scooped her up into his arms and carried her into the bedroom. She'd already pulled down the spread, so when he set her on the cool sheets, she sighed at the delightful softness caressing her back.

"I don't ever want us to be apart again," he said.

"Neither do I." She looked hard at his handsome face. "I love you, Blake Masters. I want us to be together forever."

"You took the words right out of my mouth. I am a workaholic. I hope you can deal with that."

"You could always become a detective instead of a bank manager." It was what he said he wanted to do.

"Would you like that?" he asked.

"I only want what you want."

He leaned over and kissed her quick. "Tonight is not the time to decide my future—other than making sure you're in it."

Her heart soared hearing those words. "Mmm. For that to happen though, you'll need to do something first."

Blake climbed on top of her and nabbed her nipple between his teeth. "Do you mean this?" he asked right before he switched to the other side.

"It's a good start." A really good start.

Blake worked his way down her body, making every scale under her skin light up. It was when he reached the apex of her thighs while massaging her breasts that her teeth sharpened in anticipation. This once in a lifetime event was the ultimate loving experience, one she had dreamed about for as long as she could remember. While their meeting hadn't been under the best of circumstances, it had tied them together in an intense bond.

The memory of running away from him in the woods this evening might never go away, but Greer vowed to make it up to him. The first swipe of his tongue turned her thoughts back to the moment. She arched her back in total bliss, clutching the sheets as the delicious waves of pleasure entered every cell of her body.

With Blake's fingers pinching her nipples and his tongue moving faster and faster, her climax quickly approached. Greer wanted to give Blake just as much pleasure since it wouldn't be fair to have multiple releases to his one during their mating ritual.

She ran her tongue along her sharpened teeth. "My turn," Greer panted.

He looked up. "For what?"

Blake was so cute. He was always the giver instead of a receiver. "This."

Greer scooted out from under him and pressed on his shoulder so that he'd roll onto his back. His eyes flashed teal. "This might be a bad idea," he said.

"I'll be careful."

"Care has nothing to do with it. My need for you is so out of control right now that I want to take you hard and fast right now."

Greer smiled. "That sounds wonderful, but if I don't taste you, I don't see how we can become one."

Blake reached between his legs and lifted his cock. Eyes wide in anticipation, she leaned over, released his cock from his fingers, and then went to work licking, sucking, and thoroughly enjoying making him come. The man seemed to be a pillar of restraint though. His grunts did grow louder with each lick, and she swore that a talon poked out of one of his fingers, but he never came.

Before she could pump her fist up and down again, Blake flipped her onto her back. He straddled her in a flash and then drove into her hard. Her dragon roared and rejoiced as her whole body shook with total bliss. When he kissed her, devotion and love poured out of him. He was dominant yet respectful at the same time. Only Greer didn't want that much respect. She wanted some hard core, heart-pounding loving.

With her feet firmly on the bed, she lifted her hips to meet his every thrust with one of her own while her nails dug into his skin. As he hit her sensitive spot over and over again, she had to break the kiss and drag her lips to his neck. Whether Blake followed her lead or was just overwhelmed with the same amount of lust too, she didn't know, but he placed his mouth on that soft spot between her shoulder blade and neck. Both of their scales were glowing and pulsating, creating quite a spectacular light show.

When Greer pressed her teeth against his neck, Blake hammered into her once more. They then plunged their teeth into each other's necks and held on for dear life. Heat, light, love, and lust soared through her veins. If she didn't know better, Greer would say that they had been transported to another realm, just as her ginormous orgasm claimed her.

Blake moaned, withdrew his teeth and came hard inside her, stretching her to the maximum. Greer wasn't aware of much other than believing she was floating somewhere with Blake in her arms— exactly where she wanted to be.

As if by instinct, they each licked the residue of their bite marks and then kissed the area gently.

"I wish I was better with words," Blake said. "I'd love to be able to describe what I'm experiencing right now, but I can't. It's too amazing and overwhelming."

She patted his hard ass. "No words are needed—just a few seconds of rest."

When she jerked, it implied they'd both fallen asleep. Blake slipped out of her and headed back into the bathroom where he returned with a wet washcloth.

Without a word, he cleaned her up and then himself. After tossing the cloth back into the bathroom sink, he slipped into bed and pulled her close. "Did I ever tell you that I love you?"

Greer could barely remember her own name. "I don't know, but you've shown it time and time again, and that's all that matters."

Blake hugged her hard. "We make a good pair, Greer Caspian."

She smiled, more content than she had ever been in her life. "Yes, we do."

As sleep overtook her, the image of Meena appeared, reminding her that all would be well. How right she had been.

BLAKE AWOKE A little before dawn. Not wanting to wake his sleeping beauty, he headed to the kitchen. Everything about this cabin was upscale. He even touched the kitchen counter to make sure it wasn't a figment of his imagination. It was real all right. Blake was still unsettled about who this Kenton guy was, but considering he'd led him to Greer, he'd let it go for now.

Oh, crap. Blake had kind of promised he'd let Griffin know that Greer was okay. While he only had one bar on his cell phone, it was enough to send a text. Blake told Griffin that they were staying in one of Fay's cabins and all was well. He'd let Greer spill the good news to her family about them being mated now.

Blake walked over to the large picture window and stared into the faint light edging its way between the trees. A total sense of peace surrounded him as the intermittent small flashing lights zoomed about. He suspected these were the lightning bugs Griffin had mentioned. How they could protect anyone, he didn't know, but Kenton certainly seemed to believe it too. Given the powers this man possessed, Blake decided he might be right.

Now that he and Greer were mated, he allowed himself to relax. With the ability to communicate telepathically, they could converse around others without anyone overhearing their conversation. He'd been told that if Greer experienced any pain or anxiety that he too would feel it in his bones, indicating he needed to be with her.

After a few minutes of reflection, Blake returned to the kitchen, noticing a box of peach tea on the counter. Had Greer told the fairies this was what she liked to drink, or did these special beings just know? If they were that intuitive, they'd have his special blend of hickory nut and bean coffee. Blake opened cabinet after cabinet and spotted it on the third try. Okay, that almost unsettled him.

Not one to turn down his drink of choice, he boiled some water for Greer's tea and brewed his drink in the coffee maker. As much as Blake would like to explore these woods with Greer today and pretend as if nothing had happened, he couldn't ignore the fact that the intruder from Earth was still out there.

First that ass had tried to frame Kaleena for murder, and then he had drugged both him and Greer. There must be something they could do to bring this guy to justice. After fighting with the werewolf for such a prolonged period, the man's essence was deeply embedded in Blake's mind. He wouldn't be forgetting that aura any time soon.

The Guardians had to be aware that making sure this creep didn't return to Earth was important, though after him getting away from Blake yesterday, maybe they should send him on his way. What Blake feared now was that others might follow in his path. Blake couldn't imagine having a lot of these creatures on Tarradon, all with the ability to change into anyone they chose and do whatever they wanted. Yikes.

The teapot whistled, snapping him out of his musings. He dipped the peach tea bag in a cup of boiling water and then poured himself a cup of the fresh brewed coffee.

He carried both drinks into the bedroom, set Greer's tea on the bedside table, and waited for her to rouse.

When she opened her eyes and smiled, Blake's life was complete. "Hey, sleepy head."

She rubbed her eyes. "What time is it?"

"A little after dawn. I couldn't sleep so I got up to have some coffee and made you peach tea."

She pushed up with her hands to sit up. Greer picked up the drink. "How do I know you're not a Changeling who drugged this tea?" She winked.

"Can a Changeling do this?" he telepathed.

The look on her face was precious. *"I forgot we'd be able to communicate telepathically. That's awesome."* She sipped her tea, blew out a breath, and then set it down. "Hot."

"Just the way it should be. By the way, I texted Griffin to let him know you were okay. He was worried about you."

"You had service?"

"One bar."

"I wanted to call you yesterday but had nothing."

He smiled. "It's okay. I found you." Blake sat on the edge of the bed. "What do you want to do today?"

Her lips slanted to the side. "What I want to do and what I should do are two different things. I'm worried about Kaleena. I know she is home, but what's to stop that Changeling from trying to get to her again."

She had a good point. "I take it you want to check on her?"

"Would you mind?"

Blake wouldn't mind anything Greer wanted to do, as long as he could be by her side. "Not at all. We just need to come up with a plan for eradicating this werewolf."

She clasped his arm. "We need to warn Finn and Kaleena, as well as the others that he is on the loose."

"Griffin knows. Why don't you get dressed, and we'll return so we can let Finn and the others know what we are up against in case Griffin hasn't filled them in yet."

Greer pulled back the spread. "Let's do it."

The sight of her naked body caused his dragon to roar, but he had to resist, something that was really hard to do. For the sake of the others though, he forced himself to move.

Once they'd cleaned up the cabin, they were greeted by a beautiful morning. He didn't remember the stone pathway before, but Blake had probably been overwhelmed at the time. When they reached the main path, he looked over his shoulder at Greer. While his mate was smiling, the cabin they'd just spent the night in was gone.

"Ah, Greer." Blake pointed behind her.

She spun around and froze. "Wait a minute. Where did the cabin go?"

"That's what I would like to know. We did just mate in there, right? I mean, we can communicate telepathically now, so last night really did happen."

Greer placed a hand on his chest, and Blake swore her heat went right through him. *"It most definitely did."*

Okay, they still could communicate that way. "The strange thing was when Kenton told me about the cabin, he said that I wouldn't be able to find it by myself. Maybe that's because he made it exist."

"Wait a minute. Who's Kenton?"

"He's Fay and Meena's brother."

"Good to know, but the cabin certainly existed since I had already been there a little while before you showed up."

"Maybe we stepped through a portal and didn't know it?" It was a crazy idea, but then most things that had happened recently had been totally out of this world—literally.

Greer nodded. "I can't think about this now. My head is still trying to come to grips with the mutant werewolf. Maybe Kaleena or Finn can help with what is going on."

Blake smiled. "All I know for sure is that I love you."

"Aw. I love you too. By the way, we'll need to pick up our cars on the way home."

"We can do that."

Chapter Twenty

KALEENA SQUEEZED GREER'S hand. "You and Blake didn't have to leave your little paradise to warn me. I know I have to be careful."

Blake stepped next to Greer. "We want to keep you safe."

Kaleena's eyes widened. "Look who's talking. He came after both of you. You are the ones in danger."

"We know. It's one reason why I think Greer and I should go to Earth—at least for a few days," Blake said.

The door to Kaleena's condo opened, and Finn walked in. He stepped over to his mate, gave her a hug and then a kiss. They looked into each other's eyes as if they were communicating telepathically. It was the only way it seemed to make sure the Changeling hadn't managed to become one of them again.

Finn faced them. "What did you decide?"

Greer didn't know what he was referring to. "Decide about what?"

"About what we're going to do regarding the Changeling."

Blake crossed his arms. "I don't have a plan, which is why we've been discussing taking a little trip to Earth. I want to talk with your Detective Murdoch, as well as speak to this Ophelia person. I want to see what advice she has to offer."

Greer smiled. "I think Ophelia will know how to take this guy down. I have always wanted to meet your family, Finn. Kaleena has talked about them often, and I'd love to see Silver Lake again too."

"You should join us," Blake said.

"That is a great idea," Greer telepathed. "Please do," Greer said

to Kaleena and Finn. "It will be a good emotional break. Isn't your Thanksgiving right around the corner?"

Finn smiled. "Yes, it is, and I think it's a splendid idea. Kaleena, are you up for it?"

"Are you kidding? I'll be able to get out whenever I want, and having your mom fuss after me will be quite comforting."

"Then it's settled," Finn said. He turned to Blake. "What do you hope to learn from Kalan Murdoch?"

"It's more like we need to warn him about keeping close tabs on these Changelings. We can't afford to have any more of them reach Tarradon."

Finn nodded. "I totally agree. I'll contact the bar right now to let them know they'll need to find someone to cover my shifts, but then we're free to head out."

"I'll notify the bank that I'll be taking a little vacation too."

It had all sounded so easy until they had to deal with logistics. "I'll check with Tory to see if she can work a few extra days. If she has to close the shop for a while, it won't be a big deal."

"Do we think we can get everything set up by this evening?" Blake asked.

Everyone nodded. Kaleena looked up at Finn. "I say we start packing."

BLAKE HAD NEVER been to Earth and was looking forward to the trip. Truth be told, he'd never even been through a portal before. Being with Greer, away from that evil Changeling who could transform into anyone at will, would be wonderful. He and Greer could truly enjoy each other without having to look over their shoulders all the time.

"Ready?" Greer asked.

The four of them were standing in a field. "Yes, but I don't see any portal," Blake said.

She chuckled. "That's because we haven't created it yet. Now that you're my mate, you will be able to do this too." She slipped what looked like a scale out of her pocket and swung her arm clockwise in a circle three times. She then changed directions and made two more circles. As if out of thin air, a circle of light appeared.

"That is really cool," he said, probably sounding like a geek.

"It is quite miraculous. Since we're going to Finn's house first, he'll lead the way."

"What do I need to do?" Blake asked.

"Just hold my hand and walk through the lighted circle."

Doing as Greer asked, he took maybe two steps when a blast of cold air hit him. She squeezed his hand and let go.

"We're here," Finn announced.

"Already?" Sure, she'd told him it only took a second, but he thought she'd been exaggerating.

"Yup. Come on," Finn said. "You two can stay at my place, while Kaleena and I stay with my parents."

"They won't mind if you show up this late at night?" Blake asked.

Finn smiled. "They're used to late night interruptions."

After Finn let them into his place, he showed them where he kept things. "Here's the spare phone. Just plug it in to charge it. That way, we can communicate. My number is programmed in, as is Kalan's."

"Smart thinking."

Finn winked. He and Kaleena then headed out.

Now alone, Blake turned to Greer. "Finn told us to help ourselves to the wine. We can replenish it tomorrow. Care for a glass?"

"I would love one, but what I would love more is a kiss."

Blake's heart nearly burst. He hadn't wanted to sound insensitive, but after mating with Greer, all he could think about was making love to her again. And again. "I'm not sure I can stop with one kiss."

She laughed and then wrapped her arms around his neck. "I

don't recall asking you to."

"Did I mention that I love you?"

She laughed. "Hmm. I can't remember."

"Then let me remind you by showing you how much I do."

The moment their lips pressed together, Blake's dragon roared. Scales flashed and then hardened slightly. When his teeth sharpened, he was quite sure the color of his eyes were a dead giveaway to how he felt about this truly amazing woman.

Just being away from the danger on Tarradon had his soul soaring. Blake's heart was filled with more love than he'd ever thought possible.

Greer's tongue begged for entrance into his mouth, and as he granted it, an overwhelming urge to become one with her took away all other thoughts. As if they both had the same idea at the same time, they kicked off their shoes and managed to undo their jeans and tug them down partway without breaking contact. Only because he wanted her completely naked was he willing to pull away and finish the job.

"I'm sorry I'm so needy," Blake said as he shoved off his jeans and briefs.

"No need to apologize. I've been wanting to do this all day. Now that we're here, I can't wait any longer either."

As if to prove her point, she slipped off her jacket and then removed her shirt. Her arms and chest were glowing so intensely, he bet she could light up a darkened room. Needing to have her naked and his lips on her tits, he unclasped her bra and dragged the straps down her arms.

Greer slipped his shirt over his head and tossed the material to the floor. Her panties were the last to go, and he happily removed them. They were in the cozy entranceway, and Blake saw no reason to take the time to find a bedroom.

"Come here, you," Greer said, as she wrapped her arms around his neck and plastered her breasts against his chest.

Every cell in his body sizzled. He cupped her ass and lifted her up for more access. As if it was what she'd planned all along, she wrapped her legs around his waist. Blake only had to take three steps forward before her back was pressed against the front door. The wanton nature of making love to her this way had every nerve ending lighting up as lust and desire marched through his veins.

"I can't get enough of you," Blake panted.

"Then do something about it." Greer smiled and then kissed him.

With her pussy against his cock and his emotions swamping his body, Blake's mind stopped formulating all coherent thoughts. With a quick repositioning, his cock found her entrance. As much as he wanted to take his time and taste her, his dragon was demanding some satisfaction. The first thrust sent him soaring.

Greer moaned and dragged her palms across the back of his head, their tongues dueling, tasting, and loving. Needing to be one with her, uniting their souls and their hearts, Blake slipped out and then drove into her again. And then again.

But it was Greer who seemed to need more. She planted her feet on his legs and pressed up and then dropped down, matching his rhythm, almost as if she too had been possessed by the mating draw. Her hands lowered to his shoulders right before she broke the kiss.

"Take me," she demanded.

It took a second for him to understand what she wanted, because they were already making love. She dragged her mouth to the juncture of his neck and shoulder and pressed her now sharpened teeth against his skin. The urge to do the same blocked out everything. When he was in position, he hammered into her while he drove his sharpened teeth into her neck.

From the tension rippling across his body, along with how Greer's nails were digging hard into his skin, they'd both came at the same time. Every one of his nerves fired at once, and Blake feared his dragon would finally win the war and emerge.

Don't you dare shift, he commanded.

Grrr.

He'd never known his dragon to be incapable of a coherent response before.

Blake slipped out of her, and Greer's feet slid to the floor. She stood on her toes and licked the spot where she'd bitten him, but by now the wound had almost closed up. Hers too had practically healed. Both of their dragons had done their job.

He lifted up her up and carried her into the kitchen. After a few attempts, he found a towel and cleaned them up.

"You still up for that glass of wine?" he asked.

She laughed. "Sure, as long as you don't mind carrying me to bed if I fall asleep on the sofa."

"It would be my pleasure."

THE NEXT MORNING, Greer's phone buzzed—or rather Finn's phone. She picked it up. "Hey, we got a text from Finn with directions to his parents' house," she told Blake. "He asked if we could meet with Kalan Murdoch. He's there right now."

"That was fast."

"No kidding. Uh-oh. Walking there will take too much time, so how are we going to get there? Finn took his car. It's not like we can fly. It would attract too much attention."

He grinned. "Maybe I can cloak myself, now that we've mated."

She loved his can-do attitude. "Let's give it a try." She texted Finn back saying they'd be over as soon as they were ready. She didn't know how long it would take for Blake to learn this new skill.

After dressing, they went into the backyard, which was thankfully fenced in and surrounded by trees. Even in their fifteen-foot dragon form, no neighbors could see them.

"Is there something I need to do to cloak myself?"

"I guess all I do is think about it. It's encoded in our genes."

He nodded. "Wish me luck."

Please let this work. Greer waited until Blake shifted. Three seconds later, she couldn't see him. While she could sense him, no one else would be able to. *"Good job!"* she telepathed, proud of her mate.

A few seconds later, she shifted and immediately cloaked herself. Before Blake lost focus and appeared, she took off. *"Follow me,"* she told him.

She flew over the roads since Finn had given her those directions. He must have forgotten they didn't have a car. When she spotted Finn's car in one of the driveways, alongside a Silver Lake police cruiser, she continued on, looking for a more secluded spot to land. She would have no problem setting down in her cloaked form and then shifting, but if anyone had been around, seeing two people materialize out of nowhere might be confusing and cause problems.

She located a small field not too far from his parents' place. Greer landed and shifted without her dragon form being exposed. Once on the ground, Blake immediately lost his cloak right before he shifted back.

"Maybe we should hire a cab next time," she said.

Blake looked around and chuckled. "You might be right."

It took them almost ten minutes to walk back to where she'd spotted the house. As they headed up the driveway, she tapped the hood of the cruiser. "Our guest of honor is here."

"Nervous?" Blake asked.

"I'd say more excited. I've heard so much about his parents, it's like I know them."

At the front door they knocked, and Finn greeted them. "Come in."

A scent what smelled like apple cider permeated the air. Kaleena, along with a man with long light brown hair pulled back to the nape of his neck, were seated on the sofa. He stood, walked around the coffee table, and held out his hand.

"I'm Kalan Murdoch, detective with the police department and Beta to the wolf and bear Clan here."

Greer smiled. "Greer Caspian, Kaleena's cousin. And this is my mate, Blake Masters."

Once they finished the introductions, a woman who she suspected was Finn's mom came in carrying a tray. "Thank you for suggesting Finn and Kaleena visit us. We miss them so much." The stocky woman wiped her hand on her apron and then held it out. "I'm Celia, Finn's mom. Cameron is attending to some Clan business and should be home soon. I baked you all some pumpkin spice cookies, since it's almost Thanksgiving and all."

Greer decided not to mention that Tarradon never celebrated that holiday. "Thank you."

For the next hour, the four of them shared their tales of woe about this renegade Changeling.

Kalan shook his head. "This is worse than I thought. It's enough of a nightmare that these creatures can transform into another person for a few days once a month, but to do it at will is terrifying."

Finn crunched on a cookie and then washed it down with some hot cider. "Do you know which Changeling might be the one on Tarradon?" he asked Kalan.

"I do. After Anderson came down here and we found one of his people murdered, I did a little research. Mind you I had to call in a favor to do it. I asked my brother's mate, Ainsley, to sneak into the Changeling headquarters—what there is of it—and do a little recon."

"Wasn't that dangerous?" Blake asked.

"Not too much. Ainsley has the ability to become invisible."

Blake whistled. "We could use her on Tarradon."

Kalan chuckled. "No way Jackson would let her go. Besides, who knows if her talent would work there?"

"Things do seem to be different on the two realms," Blake said.

Kalan pulled out a photo. "This is the driver's license picture of the man we believe is on Tarradon. His name is Richard Donovan, but he goes by the self-given title of Brother Richard."

Both Greer and Blake studied the photo. "This will be useful once we show it to Anderson."

"I hope so."

They'd talked a lot about what Kalan could do to make sure the

Changelings stayed where they belonged, but not what they could do to find this guy on Tarradon. "Any suggestions on how to capture this Brother Richard? Does he have any weaknesses? Something he holds dear on Earth we could use as leverage?"

"All Changelings have a weakness when around pink quartz."

Finn snapped his fingers. "I don't know why I didn't think of that before. It's their Kryptonite."

"Kryptonite?" Blake asked.

Finn chuckled. "Sorry. It's a reference to a classic television show about a superhero whose powers are diminished when near Kryptonite. It's a stone, which ironically came from his home planet of Krypton."

Greer placed a hand on Blake's arm. "Whatever the reason, if this quartz can block his powers, is there any way we can get some?"

Kalan smiled. "Funny you should ask. Our Silver Lake is lined with the stuff. I suggest you contact Ophelia, who I've been told you've met. If you do take some back to Tarradon, I can't guarantee it will permanently block all of his shifting and identity changing powers, but I've witnessed a Changeling unable to hold his shift just being near the lake. If the Changeling on Tarradon can't stay in his wolf form, he'll be easier to capture."

"I agree, assuming, as you said, this pink quartz has the same effect in our realm as it has here."

Blake clasped her hand. "True, but it's the best idea we've had yet."

"And yes, I have met Ophelia. She helped me heal Angelique."

"That's great. How about I ask Rye's mate, Izzy, to set up a meeting?" Finn asked.

Greer didn't need an intermediary. "I can contact her directly."

Blake looked over at her. *"How can you do that?"* he telepathed.

"I have a special scale that allows me to contact her. Long ago, Poppy gave it to me on one of my rare trips to Earth."

"Poppy?"

"One of those special sisters I talked about."

"You always surprise me."

Not wanting to be rude by talking with Blake telepathically, she faced the group. "I can't thank you enough, Celia, for your hospitality." She stood. "And Kalan, you are welcome any time on Tarradon."

"Thank you, but between my mate and our two kids, I have my hands full here."

"Just know that all of you are welcome to Silver Lake any time."

Finn stood and handed them the keys to his car. "I forgot I took your mode of transportation. It's too dangerous to fly."

Greer smiled. "We managed to cloak ourselves, but from now on, we'll travel the old-fashioned way. Thanks."

After they said their goodbyes, Greer and Blake headed out. Next stop: Ophelia's.

Chapter Twenty-One

"THERE SHE IS," Greer said as she slipped out of the car.

Blake stepped behind her. "She's not like I expected her to look."

"Ophelia is old. Really old." No one knew her age exactly, but if Ophelia was Poppy, Primrose, Acacia, and Magnolia's grandmother, she must be ancient.

A smile spread across Ophelia's face as she approached. "So nice to see you again, Greer." She clasped Greer's hand and squeezed it with a strength she didn't expect. Ophelia faced Blake. "And this must be your mate. Such a handsome man. Good catch." She winked.

Ophelia sure was feisty today. "We need your help."

"Let's go over to Izzy's house. It's empty, and she said I could use it whenever I wanted."

The three of them walked across the damp grass to the cobblestone pathway that led up to a cute yellow house. The door was unlocked, and Ophelia led them in. Once they were seated in the living room, Greer told her briefly about the Changeling and the trouble he'd caused.

"Oh, my, that is a shame. What can I do?"

"Finn mentioned something about the effect pink quartz has on a Changeling. He thought we could use it against this Brother Richard. We need to stop his abilities."

Ophelia smiled. "Ah yes. It's a brilliant idea to use that against him. We'll get some pink quartz and then have it fashioned into two knives. Unless you want more made."

Greer was thrilled Ophelia would help them like this.

Blake held up a hand. "Two is plenty."

"Finding him is our big concern now," Greer said.

Ophelia slapped her thighs and stood. "First things first. We're going to the lake."

"We drove if you want to ride over with us," Greer said. She had no idea if Ophelia teleported, though she knew the four sisters did.

"I'm not walking." She laughed as she headed out the front door and then turned toward the car.

Ophelia told them which way to go. A few minutes later, she pointed to a small parking lot. "This is as close as we can get with the car."

Once they exited, Ophelia led them down a tree-shaded path until a beautiful lake appeared. It's grandeur caught Greer's breath. "I've been here once before, but it never ceases to impress me."

"It is awesome. You said pink quartz lines the bottom of this lake?" Blake asked.

"Yes. The tricky part is retrieving it. Want to dive in and see if you can chip away a few pieces from the bottom?"

Blake looked over at Greer. "I'll have to shift and then go in. I can use my claws to break off a piece." He faced Ophelia. "Will that be a problem? Or should we just buy some?"

Ophelia lightly punched him in the shoulder. "No, you can't buy it. This pink quartz is special, and we like to keep a close watch on it. But no, we don't need someone spotting a dragon shifter. Give me a sec. I'll retrieve some."

The old lady was going to get it? "You don't need to do that. We'll go in."

Before Greer could stop her though, Ophelia seemed to float toward the water. It was as if she didn't feel the cold, because one minute she was on the shore walking in, and the next she had disappeared under the surface.

Blake tore off his jacket. "She won't survive under there in this cold."

Greer clasped his arm to stop him from being the hero. "Give her a second. I think she'll be okay. She's more than just some ordinary white lighter."

"I hope you're right."

They waited ten seconds. Twenty seconds. One full minute.

"Powerful white lighter or not, I'm going in," Blake said. "She has to be in trouble."

Just as Blake finished shucking off his boots and pants, Ophelia rose out of the water and floated back to shore. Blake just stared.

Ophelia smiled as she looked down at Blake's almost bare lower half. With a chuckle, she said, "I do like the reception, young man. Thank you."

Not only did Ophelia have two pieces of quartz in her hand, when she stepped onto shore, her clothes were dry. Had Greer not come from Tarradon where magic abounded, she might have freaked. Blake put on his pants and shoes and then rushed over to her.

He ran his gaze up and down Ophelia's body. "How is that possible?"

She laughed. "When you're as old as I am with ancient Wendayan powers, you'd be surprised what is possible." She waved the pink stone. "Next stop? The sword maker."

In regard to taking away this werewolf's powers, Greer believed now more than ever that what they were planning would work. Anyone who could walk into a lake, stay under water for more than a minute, and step out dry had to be a goddess. She'd seen a lot of magic in her life, but this one was at the top of the charts.

The next leg of the trip took them farther into the woods. "Who lives here?" Blake asked.

"A man by the name of Zane Barons. He's a bear shifter from Cargonia."

Greer's breath caught. "Cargonia? I can't wait to meet him. I've never been to his realm."

"A demon put a curse on him and tossed him through a portal

IGNITED BY FLAMES

where he landed in a cave. He didn't wake up for one hundred years. I believe he will be able to help. Zane creates amazing works of art out of steel and wood. He's even imbued some with magic!"

"That sounds fantastic," Greer said.

Ophelia smiled and then pointed to a cabin. "That's where he lives."

"Do you think he'll be home?" It was in the middle of the day.

"He works at the fire department, but I think he'll be there." She winked.

"Good enough." Greer was learning not to question how this woman knew so much.

When they walked up to the door and knocked, a giant of a man answered. His brows pinched for a moment, and then his face softened. "Welcome. Come in."

The next hour was like living in a dream. After explaining what they needed and why, Zane said he'd like to help.

"Come with me to my workshop," he said.

Ophelia lifted a hand. "I think I'll just wait here for you. I don't do well with dust or a lot of noise. I know what a racket some of those machines make."

Zane lowered his gaze. "Yes, ma'am. It can get pretty dirty and noisy in there. Help yourself to a drink while you wait. I'll try not to take too long."

"Thank you."

Greer and Blake followed Zane to his amazing workshop. While the materials were mostly wood, some were metal. Everything was orderly, just the way she liked it. The man definitely loved to work with his hands.

"Let me see that pink quartz." Zane held out his hand. "If it is to weaken a Changeling, I imagine you don't need the blade to be too sharp, but just in case, I'll put a silver edging on the side and sharpen it."

"That would be great," Blake said.

"I've not used this against a Changeling, but I've made a sword

179

once that took down an evil goddess."

Chelsea had told her that story. "You trained Ronan on how to defend against this demon goddess, but it was Blair Murdoch, Kalan's sister, who ended its life."

Zane grinned. "Yes. I wished I'd been able to watch that fight. The sword seemed to have taken on a life of its own."

Pride beamed off of him. He walked over to what looked like a lathe and began to shape the quartz stone. In no time, he had made two knives. The last step was to cover part of the blade with silver.

While they waited, Blake picked up a giant sword that was lying on a table. "This is amazing. Did you make this?" Blake asked.

"Yes. Try it out," Zane said.

Blake ran his fingers along the handle. "No, thanks. I'm more of a rapier kind of guy."

Greer had to work to hold in a chuckle. "You fence?"

Blake did a mock pose. "Of course. It's the job of every good rich boy to fence."

She laughed. Blake was so good at making fun of himself. "I suppose you hunt too?"

"Absolutely not. Hunting is barbaric, unless you need to feed your family. My father abhorred the sport. Archery on the other hand is a very noble sport."

"Good to know. Any other talents I should be aware of? Piano playing or ballroom dancing?" She hadn't meant to tease him, but with all this talk of killing these evil Changelings, she needed some levity.

"I have many talents that I will unfold slowly over our lifetime."

Greer smiled. "Fair enough."

The noise from some machine Zane was using drowned out any further conversation, so Greer watched the giant work. She was fascinated with the ease with which Zane skillfully crafted the blade. In less than half an hour, he handed a knife to each of them.

"I can't promise this will work on Tarradon like it does on Earth since the abilities of this Changeling seemed to have been enhanced in your realm, but it should slow him down."

"We can't thank you enough," Blake said.

"Oh, and I put a little magic into it too." He grinned.

"I don't know what to say," Blake said, as he ran his finger across the blade.

"I just want to hear that this evil Changeling isn't coming back to Earth. He and his kind have caused enough trouble."

Greer smiled. "We'll do our best."

Once they said goodbye, they gathered Ophelia and drove back to where they'd first seen her. Blake helped her out. "You've done so much for us. Can we do anything for you?" Greer asked.

She smiled. "Be there for my four granddaughters. They will all be getting a surprise next summer and might need help."

Blake clasped her hand. "We will do whatever we can."

Greer knew better than to ask her to be more specific. Poppy had mentioned that their grandmother loved to be mysterious.

After she and Blake left, they went back to Finn's parents' house to tell them they would be on their way back to Tarradon. As they knocked on the McKinnon's front door, Greer realized how sad she was that they couldn't stay.

She would have liked to spend a week going on hikes and taking pictures of the beautiful leaves that had turned every color of red, orange, yellow, and green, but she and Blake needed to take down that terrible man, Brother Richard.

"You're just in time," Finn said as he ushered them inside.

"For what?" Greer asked.

"Mom just baked some of her famous chocolate chip cookies."

Greer smiled. "Sounds divine."

They headed into the kitchen where Kaleena was chatting with Finn's mom.

Kaleena looked up and smiled. "How did it go?"

"Ophelia knew just what to do."

They showed them the special quartz knives that Zane had fashioned for them. For some reason, Greer had the sense that Ophelia would have wanted them to keep her secret about her ability to walk into the lake, and how after retrieving the pink quartz from the bottom, she'd emerged dry. For all Greer knew though, Ophelia put a spell on them, and they just thought she'd walked into the water.

"You look like you're ready to leave," Kaleena said with longing in her voice.

Because of Kaleena's condition, Finn said they would be staying put for a while—at least until the Changeling had been dealt with.

"We had intended to take a small vacation, but I feel guilty being here when that maniac is on the loose," Greer said. "If we didn't have a good chance of taking him down, we would remain here."

Finn wrapped an arm around Kaleena's shoulder. "I would say to leave it to the cops, but they don't have the skills. Those knives are the best chance we have of ridding Tarradon of that Changeling. If it works, Kalan might want to have Zane make more for him and his men."

Greer smiled. "Sounds great."

Kaleena placed her hands on her stomach. "We will return if our little dragon acts up, which he or she is right now."

"Let me help." Greer placed her hands on Kaleena's stomach and sent her calming thoughts to the baby.

Kaleena sighed. "Much better. Thank you."

Greer didn't want to leave, but her Guardian honor told her it was the right thing to do. They said their goodbyes, thanked Mrs. McKinnon for her hospitality, and then left. They drove back to Finn's house where they left the car keys and his phone on the dining room table before stepping into the back yard, away from prying eyes.

Greer held out a scale. "Do you want to try to make a portal?"

Blake's eyes widened. "Me?"

"You are one of us now. It's easy—three times to the right and then two to the left. We'll both picture your rooftop. It will give us some leeway in case our aim is off."

"You mean in case *my* aim is off."

She smiled. "We'll hold hands to make sure we land in the same spot."

"Okay, here goes."

Blake followed the instructions exactly, and to both of their delights, the portal formed. One step later, they were on the bank's roof.

"That is so cool," Blake said. "Can I go anywhere I can imagine?"

"Yes, but we try not to abuse the system. You remember Mange, right?"

Blake laughed. "Of course."

"It's possible he snuck in through the portal when Angelique came to Tarradon."

Blake spun around. "Could anyone else be here now?"

Greer slipped her arm through his. "I doubt it, but we can never be too sure when we Guardians create a portal for ourselves."

"I'll be sure to keep you by my side then."

She smiled. "Perfect." They had just entered Blake's apartment when her cell rang. "So much for having any downtime." Greer checked the caller ID. "It's Declan."

"Are you back?" he asked.

"Blake and I just returned. What's up?"

"We had an attempted break in at the mines."

Declan wouldn't have called unless it involved the Changeling. "I'm going to put you on speaker so Blake can hear." She pressed the button. "Did you catch him?"

"No, but I think you and Blake might like to see the footage."

"Are you at the Caspian mine office right now?"

"Yes."

Blake's brows furrowed. "We'll be right over," he said. "Do you think it's the Changeling?" Blake asked once she disconnected.

"We'll find out soon enough."

Chapter Twenty-Two

DECLAN REPLAYED THE video of the wolf sniffing around. "It's almost comical," Greer's cousin said. "I'm guessing he was trying to find some sardonyx."

"That would be my guess too," Blake said. "My favorite part, and maybe the scariest, is when the wolf looks right into the camera and we can see his eyes glowing red."

"And the worst is when he shifts, since he's naked. I can't unsee that," Greer responded. Both men laughed. "Could you see his essence trail?" she asked Blake.

"No. I need to be there in person for that."

She reached out and clasped his hand. "Your talents are still wonderful."

Declan cleared his throat, possibly embarrassed by the flirty exchange that had just passed between them. "Here comes the good part. Our security guard charges in. The Changeling takes one look at him, shifts, and races off."

"Why didn't your man shoot?" Blake asked.

Declan shook his head. "He told me that when he saw a naked man, he was so taken aback that he kind of froze. Then the man ran off. To be honest, we often get people in here hoping to find some gems lying on the ground. I don't think they have any idea that we need to process and polish them first."

"I bet. When was this feed taken," Blake asked.

"About eight hours ago," Declan said.

Crap. "He could be anywhere by now," Greer said.

"We know he's still on Tarradon, right?" Blake had such hope in his voice.

"Yes. We could do a sweep of the area, but if he is in his wolf form, from high in the sky we won't be able to tell if it's an ordinary wolf or a Changeling," Declan said.

"We have his driver's license photo," Greer said. "I'll ask Anderson to circulate his picture. We might find him that way."

"Give it to me and I'll let everyone know," Declan said. "You can take to the skies."

"Eight hours is a long time for an essence trail to still be around, but if there is any of it there, I'll know." Blake then turned to Greer. "Want to join me?"

"Absolutely."

They left the Caspian mining office and headed out to the back mine where this intruder had been spotted. They landed and shifted.

"Anything?" she asked.

"I see a wisp of light here and there, but I can't get a read on which way he went. It would have been better if he'd been in one area for a longer period of time."

That was a bit disappointing. "Maybe it will be stronger where he tried to get into the building. I can't believe that guy would actually think we'd leave the place unsecured though."

"Desperate people do desperate things." Blake held out his hand. "I see something. Wait here."

"No problem." Greer didn't want to be the one to mess things up.

Blake shifted into his dragon form again and soared upward. Greer watched him rise and then dive, searching the area in what looked like a grid pattern.

"I found something," he telepathed, sounding excited. *"Join me."*

Greer shifted and was by his side a few seconds later. *"What did you see?"*

"I can tell that the trail is heading west. Care to see where it leads?"

"Of course." Both of them had their pink quartz knives just in case they ran into Richard Donovan in the flesh.

She couldn't wait to tell the Changeling that she knew his name. Greer was equally anxious to see just how much their knives would affect the werewolf's abilities. After they took care of this intruder, they would give one of the knives to Anderson so that he could keep the Changeling under control. The other knife they would give to Kalan Murdoch to protect him against the rest of the Changeling Clan back on Earth. While he could have another knife made, it might not contain the level of magic hers had been imbued with.

"This way," Blake telepathed, sounding excited.

They flew toward the forest, though she wasn't sure if Blake planned to go in on foot. Surely, Richard Donovan wouldn't be in the same campsite as before. After the failed attempt at getting more sardonyx from the Caspian mines, she would have thought he'd want to head back to Earth. Too bad, he'd never succeed.

Greer flew side by side with Blake, refraining from conversation. She understood his need to concentrate. When they reached the forest edge, Blake slowed down.

"I've lost the trail in the foliage. I want to take a swing over the outer edge just in case he exited somewhere."

"Should we split up?" Even though they had mated, it didn't appear as if she'd inherited his ability to sense a person's essence trail. Hopefully with some practice, she might learn how.

"How about if you take that open space over there and I'll do another pass over the forest? Even if you only think you see something, let me know right away. I don't want you to try to take down that scum by yourself."

Greer bit back a retort. She could take down that ass of a Changeling even when not in her dragon form—assuming the knife would keep his powers at bay. *"Sounds good."*

Clearly on a mission, Blake took off toward the forested area, flying just above the treetops. She wondered if he could see a trail of light in between all the dense foliage. Greer shot eastward toward the castle grounds, though just being near the Royals made her sick. Cloaking herself, she flew close to the ground, keeping a keen eye out for any werewolves. If—and that was a big if—Richard Donovan hadn't changed into someone else, she might be able to identify him from this vantage point.

Greer had surveyed the fields in front and in back of the castle and was about to return to where Blake was when a black Royal dragon rounded the corner with a naked human in its claws. Aha!

The dragon landed and dropped the sought-after Changeling onto the grass close to the castle entrance. The guard shifted. When Greer hovered next to them, the man had the face of Richard Donovan. Bingo!

"Blake, I found him. I'm at the north end of the grassy area close to the castle."

"Great. I'll be right there."

Greer landed, but remained cloaked in her dragon form. The werewolf approached the guard. "Why did you nab me?" Donovan crossed his arms over his chest and lifted his chin.

"You know why. You violated your promise to Prince Omar."

"Fuck Prince Omar. I set up Kaleena Sinclair just as he'd asked. I even planned to deliver her cousin to him, but another dragon found us."

Okay, that was interesting. Her ass of a cousin Prince Omar was behind all of this. Her own capture however, seemed to be something Donovan thought up himself.

"I don't care about your excuses. Walk."

The werewolf didn't move. "I'm not going back to that cell."

"We'll see about that."

He'd been imprisoned? Nothing was making much sense. While the Royals might keep this Changeling behind bars, she didn't trust the werewolf not to touch a guard and pretend to be him. It was time for a little intervention.

Right before she revealed herself, the werewolf shifted into his animal form and took off toward the woods. Crap.

"I've got this," Blake telepathed, as she sensed him overhead.

"Be careful."

A second castle guard appeared, landed, and then shifted.

"Go after him," the first guard commanded the newcomer.

Greer shifted and appeared. "Stop!"

They froze, probably trying to figure out why they hadn't even sensed her. "We'll take care of Richard Donovan," she announced.

"We?"

"My mate is in the woods as we speak, ready to take him down." She hoped that was the truth.

"We have our orders, ma'am."

She liked the title, but she sensed he had no idea who she was. Greer and her whole family disliked and distrusted the royal family. Sure, the queen, who was merely a pawn in the royal game, was her aunt, but the rest of the family was evil. "I'll speak with my aunt, the queen."

"Your aunt?"

"Yes, or would you rather I tell my cousin Omar how you had the opportunity to bring in that scoundrel Donovan and failed?" Sure, she was bluffing since she had no intentions of ever speaking to the unethical prince again, but they couldn't know that.

The men exchanged glances. "Who did you say you were?

Greer had said too much to back down now. "Greer Caspian. My mother, Iona, is Queen Teresa's sister." She puffed out her chest for effect.

"*Found the sniveling weasel,*" Blake telepathed, taking her focus off the two guards for a moment.

"*Do what you need to do. I'm trying to reason with two Royal Guards, but I don't think I can hold them off for much longer. They want the werewolf, so please be fast.*"

"*I will be.*"

The second guard stepped forward. "We'll take our chances. We need to capture that werewolf. He's dangerous."

"You're telling me. He drugged and kidnapped me. Fortunately, my mate came and scared him off."

The second guard smiled. "Thank you for that information.

Now, if you'll excuse us, we have a werewolf to retrieve." They both shifted.

Greer wasn't going to let them fight Blake to get that horrible little Changeling. Chances were, the sneaky werewolf would find a way to escape. She shifted, cloaked herself again so that they couldn't detect her whereabouts, and soared upward toward the two beasts.

She didn't want to kill them, just stall them a bit. Surprise was on her side when she rammed her head against the wing of the first dragon, causing him to tilt to the side. While effective, it would only take him a few seconds to recover.

In the meantime, she flew after the second dragon and was able to align herself over him before running a claw down his wing. He shrieked and then dove toward the ground.

As much as she could use help from Blake, he needed to capture the Changeling. No way did she want that werewolf to escape again. He'd done enough damage on Tarradon. Prince Omar might not care that this Earthling had killed several people, but she did.

Greer must have been too focused on the Changeling's plight and on the second dragon's cries, because her cloaking flickered on and off. The next thing she knew, sharp claws dug into her back.

Damn it. Needing to save energy, she uncloaked herself and then did a slight roll to dislodge his talons. She failed.

"Are you all right?" came Blake's voice into her head.

"I'll be fine. Kill the Changeling." She worked to keep the pain from her voice.

"I'm trying."

Greer didn't feel any pain radiating off of Blake, so she had to assume he hadn't been injured. She rocked right and then left, finally managing to get out of the dragon's grasp. The first wing flap caused pain to streak up her back. That dragon's claws must have hit a nerve.

Her mind spun, trying to figure out the best way to defeat these two. As she leaned to the side to check them out, the second dragon she'd initially injured charged, shooting fire in her face. While her scales would repel the heat, the flames hindered her vision.

As much as she'd like to disappear and fly off, at this point, she doubted these two would let her. They were probably thinking they'd be rewarded for killing a Caspian.

Sucking up what energy she had left, Greer spewed out a stream of her own fire at her attacker. Unfortunately, he dodged her flames.

The two dragons lined up next to each other and sped toward her. At the last minute, she dove under them before soaring above, a trick Thane had taught her. Twisting around, Greer snagged the wing of the first dragon. His squeals caused his partner to charge her. When his talons stabbed her neck, her vision blurred, and her energy poured out of her.

For no reason, the dragon above her let go and flew off. She wanted to go after him, but her ability to fly had been compromised. Both dragons were getting away, heading toward the forest. Shit. Then a wave of familiarity assaulted her. When she spun around, her heart soared.

Griffin was here! How in the world did he know where to find her? Right now, it didn't matter. He was attacking one of the dragons. A second later, that animal went limp and dropped to the ground. The other dragon turned around and sped toward the castle. Coward. Not that she could blame him since Griffin was an imposing figure.

She managed to land, and Griffin set down a moment later. Only after she shifted did she realize she should have stayed in her dragon form a little longer, but she needed to make sure Blake was okay.

"I should ask what you are doing here, but whatever the reason, I'm glad you came. I need to see if Blake is okay first. He's fighting the Changeling."

"You would know if he'd been injured."

"Are you okay?" came Blake's voice into her head.

"I am now. Griffin came and saved the day. We're on our way to you."

"Good."

She turned to Griffin. "How did you happen to be here?"

"I'll tell you on the way."

As soon as they entered the forest, Greer jogged when she could, and walked when the pain increased too much. "Talk to me."

"Danita had a premonition. She saw you fighting the Royal Guards and that you looked to be in trouble."

"I didn't know she was psychic."

"Neither did I, but I'm glad I believed her."

Greer smiled. "Me too. Please thank her."

"Trust me, I will."

Chapter Twenty-Three

W ITH THE KNOWLEDGE that Greer was okay, Blake lifted his pink quartz knife and swung it at the Changeling. If the last few minutes of battling with him was any indication, the man was a well-trained fighter. The werewolf had managed to avoid serious injury, but that was about to end. For his own sense of fair play, Blake had wanted to keep it a level fight. He could have shot fire at the naked man and burned him to a crisp, but that wasn't Blake's style.

Apparently, when Blake nicked the man's arms and legs a few times, the quartz had short-circuited the werewolf's ability to shift. He'd cursed of course, but Blake wasn't going to let him escape again. No, this Changeling wasn't going to get away ever again.

"Ready to give up?" Blake asked.

"Fuck you."

A wave of powerful desire blasted him, taking his mind off the capture. Leaves rustled and sticks crunched. If it hadn't been for the lust, he wouldn't have even considered that Greer was near. The two sets of foot steps meant she was with Griffin. Good.

The werewolf managed to extend his claws—something he hadn't been able to do before, or so Blake thought—and swiped a path of destruction across Blake's chest.

"That's it!" Blake shouted.

He lunged and thrust the knife at the werewolf's face. Richard Donovan twisted to get out of the way of the blade, but instead of avoiding the sharp strike to the head, it caused Blake's knife to cut open the man's throat. Donovan's eyes widened. He clasped his neck and staggered backward.

Blake's goal had only been to injure the man in order to make it easier to carry him to the police station. From the way the blood was gushing out of the man's artery, Blake would be calling the coroner instead to take away the body.

Greer rushed up to Blake, and Griffin was right behind her. She threw herself into his arms, and he hugged her tight, only to let go a few seconds later when he felt wounds on her back. "You're injured."

She leaned away from him. "My dragon will heal me, but you're injured too."

"Just a scratch." Blake looked over at Griffin. "Thanks for coming, but why are you here?"

"Greer will fill you in." He looked down at the dying man. "I don't think he has much longer to live. I need to contact Anderson and have him come and deal with this man. You need to take Greer back so she can heal fully."

"I will."

"Now go. I'll catch up to you guys later."

Blake stepped over to her brother and hugged him. "Thanks for helping Greer."

"She did most of the work. I was just the clean-up guy."

Not wanting to be anywhere near the Royal property, they walked down the pathway in the opposite direction as the castle, hoping to find an opening in the trees where they could take off.

"Tell me what happened," Blake said. "Clearly, you were injured."

"It's not a big deal—mostly because Griffin showed up at the perfect time. I was trying to stall two dragons, since they wanted to go after the Changeling. I had the upper hand until I didn't."

"I know what that's like, but tell me exactly how Griffin knew you were in trouble?"

She explained about Danita having a vision of her being attacked.

"I haven't met Danita yet. I take it she's psychic?"

"Apparently, this is a new thing for her. A while back, she was held captive by a dark lighter for weeks and subjected to a lot of darkness. I've been told it can change a person. Maybe it is only now manifesting itself."

"Whatever caused her to know you were in trouble, I'm glad she contacted Griffin."

"You and me both."

"If I ever meet her, I'll be sure to thank her for sending Griffin to your rescue. I felt your pain when you were injured, and I wanted to go to you, but that would mean losing our psycho killer."

Greer clasped his hand and squeezed. "You were right to finish off that evil Changeling. I'm sorry you couldn't take him in. I know you didn't want to kill him outright."

"I didn't, but I can't say I'm sorry he's gone." Light from the sun shot through a break in the trees. "Hey. We can take off from here. Are you good to fly?"

She smiled. "Now that I'm with you, my dragon has done wonders."

Greer shifted and shot straight up to the bright sky above, and Blake followed suit. He worried about some of the wounds he saw on her back, but after a few minutes of flying, he bet her dragon would be able to heal her.

A short while later, they both landed on the rooftop of the bank and shifted. He rushed over to her. "How are you feeling and be honest?"

"Tired but fine. Are you sure that Changeling is dead?"

"You saw him. I cut his throat. He might have been alive when we left, but he won't last long." Blake pulled the knife out of his pocket. Traces of red were still on the tip.

Greer rubbed his arm. "I know you did everything you could not to kill him."

"Probably not everything. When I thought about what grief his being here had caused you and so many others, he deserved to die."

She held out her hand. "Let's forget about that for now. How about taking a shower with me? I could certainly use one."

Blake wove his fingers through hers. "It would be my pleasure."

GREER STOOD NEXT to Blake on top of the bank building, suitcases in hand. "Ready?"

He inhaled and then blew out a breath. "Ready."

They'd already given one of the special knives to Anderson in the event another Changeling ever made it through the portal. Now they were on their way back to Silver Lake, Tennessee to tell Kaleena that all was safe and to present the second pink quartz knife to Detective Murdoch.

This time they wanted to stay a few days, or maybe even longer, in order to enjoy the countryside and each other. Finn had told them that if they wanted to hike, he could tell them about a few paths, but if they were interested in antique shopping or looking at handmade crafts, he could direct them there too.

All Greer really wanted was to be with Blake when the world wasn't trying to harm them. After discussing at length where they wanted to go, they decided they would rent an RV and explore the US.

Greer handed Blake her dragon scale. "Go ahead. Picture Finn's parents' house, and then make the wide circles."

"I'll do my best." He made his circles big, going clockwise and then counterclockwise. When the portal appeared, Blake almost jumped. "I did it again! I'm getting good at this."

Seeing him happy was the best present he could give her. "You are, now hold my hand."

They picked up their suitcases and stepped through the portal, which promptly disappeared the moment they crossed it. They probably shouldn't have landed where anyone could have seen them, but because it was dark, she hoped no one would notice them appear out of nowhere.

They hoofed it up to the front door of Finn's parents' home and knocked.

Mrs. Murdoch answered. "You're back! How wonderful. Come in, come in." She turned halfway around. "Finn. Kaleena. Guess who's here?"

When she spotted Kaleena coming out of the kitchen, Greer's heart soared.

Kaleena opened her arms. "You're back so soon!"

Greer couldn't help but smile. "Yes, and we have a story to tell you both."

For the next half hour, they detailed how they'd battled against the Royal Guards, and then eventually scared them off, thanks to Griffin's help.

"This Changeling was given orders by our cousin to frame me for murder?" Kaleena asked.

"Apparently."

"What a fucktard," Kaleena whispered. "I don't know why I'm surprised though. After all, his own brother had me kidnapped."

Blake wrapped an arm around Greer's waist. "Nice family you have there—and I'm talking about the Royals, of course."

"Tell me about it." It stuck in her craw every time her uncle and cousins acted so selfishly.

Finn moved closer to Kaleena as if he wanted to protect her, even though the Changeling was dead. "I guess it's safe to return now." He faced his mate. "What do you think? Want to go home?"

She sighed. "As much as I love being here, we both have obligations back on Tarradon."

"I know." He turned to Greer and Blake. "What are you guys going to do? Head back to Tarradon too?"

Blake slipped the quartz knife from his backpack. "I want to give this to your Detective Murdoch. It may come in handy against the other Changelings."

Finn grinned. "That's awesome. Then what?"

Greer looked up at Blake. "From the first moment we met, one of us—either alone or together—has been attacked, drugged, kidnapped, or put in jail, fighting for our lives, or chasing after evil beings."

"That includes Mange, and that was even before this Changeling from Earth arrived," Blake added.

"So we're going to take a little vacation because we deserve one," Greer said.

Finn grinned. "You most certainly do. Where are you planning to go?"

"As beautiful as Silver Lake is, we thought we'd rent an RV here and head west. How long we'll be gone or where we'll end up isn't important right now. This will be a time to build the beautiful connection Blake and I already have started as mates."

Kaleena hugged her again. "I am so happy for you."

"Me too."

"I can hook you up with someone who rents RV's," Finn said. "He owes our family a few favors. He'll overlook your lack of a driver's license but don't get pulled over. No telling what the cops would do."

Greer smiled. "I hadn't even thought about that, but I'm sure Blake will be extra careful. As for the RV, we want to be able to leave it somewhere between here and California. We'll then find a secluded spot and portal home."

"Sounds good. I'll give Stan a call."

"That would be awesome. Would you mind if we stay one more night at your place?" Greer asked.

"No problem. You're welcome to use my spare phone too. Just give it back when you return to Edendale."

"That's perfect."

"Do you need me to drive you to my place?"

Greer nodded. "That would be great."

"Let me call my friend about the RV, and then I'll take you over."

"It's almost past ten at night."

He waved a hand. "Stan won't mind." Less than five minutes later, Finn returned from some back room. "It's all set. I'll take you there now to do the rental agreement. I'll use my credit card and you guys can pay me back in Denlars."

"That's so nice of you. Are you sure we can get the RV now?"

"Yup. As I said Stan owes my family a lot of favors."

Greer hugged him. "You are the best."

"Keep reminding Kaleena of that."

Finn was being silly. "Trust me, she knows," Greer said.

After another round of farewells, Finn drove them to town where they picked out an RV. To their delight, this vehicle came from Arizona. Not that they planned to necessarily go that far, but it was nice to know they could rent in one place and drop it off at another.

Once all of the papers were signed, Blake pocketed the keys from the manager. "We can drive it back to your house, Finn. You go back and make sure Kaleena is fine." Blake held out his hand. "We can't thank you enough."

"Are you kidding? You rid the realm of one bad Changeling. That's thanks enough."

He had a point. Greer hugged Finn once more. "See you on the other side."

As soon as Finn took off, she and Blake climbed into the RV. While it wasn't super big, it had everything they would need for a great journey. While not being able to fly was a bummer, this way at least they could experience Earth like everyone else.

Back at Finn's house, the moment they stepped inside, Greer finally felt free and secure, just before waves of lust assaulted her. For so long, both of them had been on guard against that Changeling and the dark entities. Now they were anonymous and safe.

Greer peeled off her jacket and kicked off her shoes. "How about getting comfortable?"

Blake stalked toward her. "I plan to get *real* comfortable. Greer Caspian, you turn me on something fierce."

He drew her close and kissed her, causing every hormone in her body to flare with desperation. Every fiber of her being needed him. Now. She pressed her chest against his and walked him backward until his back hit the front door. Greer broke the kiss. "I want you naked."

Blake smiled. "Someone's in a hurry."

Her eyes widened. "Aren't you?"

"More than in a hurry, but I don't want you to think I can't keep a level head around you."

"Is that so, Mr. Control? Think about it. We're mates. And animals. So, let's act like it." She licked her lips, acting very out of character, but loving it at the same time.

Blake laughed. "Not that I'm complaining in the least, but where did the prim and proper Greer Caspian go?"

"She disappeared the moment I met you."

Blake cupped her face and kissed her. "Mmm."

"How about showing me how much you appreciate my transformation?" she asked.

He grinned. "I do love a challenge."

He kicked off his shoes and slipped off his jacket before dragging down his pants and briefs. Greer whistled. "That's what I'm talking about."

He lifted off his shirt and dropped it on the ground. "Better?"

"Much."

Naked, he clasped her to his chest, sending her to another realm. Pleasure, bliss, and pure joy filled her as she lowered her pants.

"Let me help." He dropped to his knees and dragged her jeans and panties off. "I've been dreaming of this for so long."

She laughed. "It hasn't been that long."

"You want to bet? Even five minutes is too long."

Greer sure did love this man. When he widened her legs and swiped a tongue across her clit, she soared. Her breath increased, and her talons tried to force themselves to the surface.

Be good, she demanded of her dragon.

Then you better hurry. The thought of totally focusing on the two of you for the next few days excites me too much.

Greer dug her nails into Blake's shoulders and closed her eyes, loving how her mate could transport her with little effort. Waves of delight darted up her body, causing her inner dragon to scrape and claw. More than anything, Greer wanted to return the favor.

"My turn."

Blake seemed to ignore her, his moans growing louder and more forceful by the second. His tongue kept flicking across her opening as his hands squeezed her butt. It didn't seem as if he would stop. Not that she really wanted him to, but Blake deserved some pleasure too. She was the first to admit though that he seemed to be enjoying himself just fine.

When his tongue delved into her opening, she lost it. Her climax swooped in, causing her knees to nearly buckle.

Keeping a good grasp on her, Blake stood. "You liked that."

"I loved that, but now it's my turn."

"You know my opinion on that when I'm too excited," he said.

Greer laughed. "You aren't going to deny me my pleasure, are you?"

"Never."

Blake cupped her face and then lifted her up. "I thought you were the one who mentioned getting comfortable."

"So I did." He carried her to the bedroom. Together, they land-ed on the bed with him on top of her. "My turn to see if I can excite you the way you turned me on," she said.

"In a moment." Blake kissed her. He seemed desperate, if the way he was touching her and probing her with his tongue was any indication.

Her tongue battled for position. With her breasts against his chest, Greer ran her hands down his muscled back. Wow. How did she get so lucky to find this amazing man? Okay, Fate might have had a hand in that.

When his hard cock dug into her belly, she abandoned all thoughts of how she'd gotten so lucky to land Blake Masters. Now she wanted more, which meant she wanted all of him.

Greer turned the aggressor. She pushed on his shoulder to roll him over. She'd planned on sucking his cock, but seeing him this way made her need even greater.

"I want you so bad," he said as his eyelids fluttered closed. "Ride me."

"You don't have to ask twice." Greer straddled him.

Blake grabbed his dick and slid it into her wet opening. Wild desire assaulted her as his cock tunneled straight to the end. Her breath caught, and her heart pounded. This insane urge to have him made her realize what she'd been missing her whole life—Blake Masters.

She lifted up and then dropped back down. Blake pushed up on his elbows just far enough for his lips to capture one of her nipples. The pressure sent her soaring in so many ways. Passion and lust overwhelmed her. Gone was her usual composed state. Greer seemed to have entered a world of desire and love, all rolled into a hot package she called Blake.

As he pounded into her, her teeth sharpened, her scales glowed bright, and her talons peeked through the tips of her fingers. In one quick move, he flipped her off him and withdrew. Before she knew what was happening, he had her up on her hands and knees. He then palmed her breasts as he hammered into her. The change in pressure pushed her really close to the edge. It was when he dragged his lips down her neck, across to that sensitive spot, and sank his fangs into her that fireworks exploded—at least in her mind they did. Both of them climaxed and their bodies pulsed.

The added rush of endorphins swamped her, making her muscles almost useless. She lowered her head and then collapsed onto the bed. Blake held her for a minute and then slipped out.

"Let me find something to clean us up with."

She didn't know where he went, but he returned with a warm cloth and handed it to her. "You up for a shower?" he asked.

"Give me a minute. You overwhelmed all of my senses."

He leaned over and kissed her. "I'm glad I did."

Greer wrapped her arms around his neck. She patted his back and then sat up. "Did I tell you I love you?"

"Hmm. It's so hard to recall when the most beautiful woman in the world is naked in front of me."

"You do know how to make a woman feel good and loved."

"Only you."

Blake lifted her off the bed and carried her into the bathroom. These next few weeks were going to be amazing.

I hope you enjoyed reading Greer and Blake's story as much as I enjoyed writing it.

Don't forget to sign up for my newsletter *to receive three free books, as well as up-to-date information on my stories. If you prefer to only receive notices regarding my releases, follow me on BookBub.*

http://smarturl.it/VellaDayNL

bookbub.com/authors/vella-day

If you'd like a FREE bonus scene of Greer and Blake's travel in their RV, go to the link: https://dl.bookfunnel.com/iyzay8vmln

Next up is Griffin and Danita's story. Here is a sneak peek of the first chapter.

"ARE YOU STILL having nightmares?" Danita Warren's therapist asked.

Why did Dr. Aminor always insist on digging into that wound? She had more pressing things to discuss with her therapist though.

Danita rubbed the worn wooden chair arm in the doctor's rather dark office. "Yes. Every night like clockwork."

Her brows rose as she leaned forward. "And? Are they less scary, more scary, longer or shorter in duration that when they first started?"

Danita huffed, hating herself for being so weak. "Ever since that terrible wolf attacked me a few days ago, it's been worse. The strange part is that I don't see his red eyes staring down at me like I would have thought, but rather those of Sanditra's." Sanditra—that horrible dark lighter who tried to turn Danita's light into darkness.

"Knowing she is dead doesn't seem to help, does it?" her therapist asked as she made a note on her tablet.

"No."

"Why is that do you suppose?"

"Because I am partially evil. She altered the light inside me when she made me do those despicable acts."

Dr. Aminor added another note. "And why do you think you are evil? Have you done bad things?"

"Not yet, but I can feel some kind of darkness welling up inside me at random times." Danita looked up. "I had a premonition recently—something that has never happened before."

Her doctor's eyes sparkled with interest. "A premonition? This is new. What was it about?"

Danita blew out a breath. "After my recent wolf attack, this woman, Greer Caspian, came and helped heal me from my wounds.

It was a few days later that I pictured her in trouble. When I told her brother about it, he charged out and was able to save her."

Her therapist smiled. "That sounds like a good thing. You helped saved the woman who helped you! I wouldn't call that being dark at all!"

"You might think so, but my insides felt as if they were on fire, and I'm not sure why."

"I wouldn't worry about you being evil until you start doing evil deeds. Helping someone else shows that your white light is still strong."

"I hope so."

"Tell me again about this recurring nightmare."

"Why? It's always the same—Sanditra is making me do evil things."

Dr. Aminor waved her stylus at Danita. "Yes, but you remember something different each time. I think when we have all of the pieces, we'll be able to make more sense of it."

Danita doubted that, but she'd try to recall what last night's dream was about. "One minute I'm in my usual cell in the Royal castle, the handcuffs sending poison through my body, and the next I am outside in the dark."

"Then what happens?"

"Sanditra is looming over me with that insidious smile of hers that cuts me to the core. I swear that dark lighter bitch could always see right through me." Danita huffed. "She starts off being nice and then turns really cruel."

"During this dream, you don't know in your heart that she is dead?"

"Not really. It's probably because I know she is too evil to be gone for good."

"We've talked about this, you know."

Danita blew out another breath, not appreciating Dr. Aminor's slightly condescending tone. It didn't matter if she was trying to be helpful. "I know."

"Did Sanditra force you to perform dark magic last night in your dream?"

"Surprisingly, no. She came, laughed uncontrollably for a minute, and then just left. It was strange."

"How did that make you feel?"

Danita wanted to lash out at the therapist for asking that way too obvious question. "Scared the white light right out of my body." Fear had actually paralyzed her to the point where she couldn't move, not even while asleep.

"Then what happened?"

Danita clenched her fists to keep them from shaking. "Evil thoughts bombarded me."

"What did you want to do?" Aminor asked, her words metered.

"Kill someone. And before you ask who, I don't know, but I suspect it was some Royal for taking me. Then again, it could be Sanditra for ruining me. I woke up in a sweat, my body trembling and my heart racing."

"You were scared."

Why did she have to state the obvious? "Yes. I'd never had that exact dream before—or those horrible feelings of such rage."

"What did you do to compensate for these evil thoughts?" the doctor asked.

"What you suggested. I pictured myself before I had been kidnapped by the Royals." Danita closed her eyes and entered that pleasant sphere right then. "My safe place is on top of this hill where the pink, yellow, and white wild flowers abound. I imagine being on my back staring up at the bright blue sky watching the clouds float by and listening to the birds go about their business. The scene calms me and brings out my light." She reopened her eyes.

Dr. Aminor was actually smiling. "Excellent. Keep doing that." Just as quickly she sobered. "I think this recent werewolf attacked has set you back."

She shook her head. "The attack was painful, sure, but this woman Greer healed me rather quickly. I think it's because I'm still upset over my cousin's recent disappearance that I have them. Every time I think about where Wendy could be, these extra dark feelings emerge."

"That's maybe why you've been picturing yourself with Sanditra during the night. The darkness could represent your feeling of helplessness."

Way to make me feel worse! "It would seem so."

"So no progress on learning about Wendy's whereabouts?"

Danita's stomach churned at not only the possibly of losing her beloved cousin and friend, but at losing control over her own thoughts. "No. Nothing."

Dr. Aminor scribbled something on her tablet. "It has to be hard, but you can fight through it. How are you handling these feelings of despair? Besides coming here, of course or picturing yourself on top of a mountain in a field of flowers?"

"I try to think of positive thoughts as much as I can, but I fail miserably most of the time. To be honest, I'm increasingly angry with each passing day. That wolf attack was just the final straw I think. Anyone would be upset if her only relative had gone missing. I believe what would help me the most is doing something to find her. Clearly, the police have failed. It's been over a week since Wendy has disappeared."

"Danita, please. We've spoken about this. If your cousin was abducted, you need to leave it to the authorities to find her."

Danita's lip uncontrollably curled. "They haven't done a damned thing! A week is a long time to be held captive. I should know!" She was almost shouting.

"Calm down. This isn't helping to bring back the rest of your white light."

It was the reason why she was in therapy in the first place. "I know, but it's so frustrating. Wendy is the only family I have. She's sweet. Kind. This never should have happened to her. What could anyone want with her?"

"Tell me what you do know."

Facts helped center her, and Aminor knew that. "Nothing more than what I told the cops and Griffin Caspian." Ah, Griffin. He'd been the one she'd called after that terrible wolf attack in the woods. Within minutes, he was by her side, flying her to safety. He'd also been the one who had helped her after her escape from the Royal prison. She wouldn't have recovered this much if it hadn't been for him. "Wendy's neighbor heard a commotion in the apartment above hers—where Wendy lives. Normally, my cousin is super quiet since she works on her articles during the day. She's a journalist. At first, the neighbor thought Wendy was moving furniture, but then she heard a shout followed by a thud. The neighbor is elderly and wasn't about to run to the rescue, so she went next door to speak to her neighbor—only he wasn't home. She went back inside and called the police."

"What did they find?"

"A lamp had been turned over, and a shattered coffee cup was on the floor," Danita said. "Two pillows were also slashed. That seemed rather random to me, but I think they were trying to make it look like a robbery."

"And Wendy?"

"She was nowhere to be found."

"It appears as if she put up a good fight."

"Wendy is a wolf shifter, so I'm hoping she did some damage to her kidnapper or kidnappers." It was the only scenario that made sense.

"Has there been a ransom note or contact of any kind?" Aminor asked very matter-of-factly.

She shook her head. "Wendy and her dad are estranged. Besides, he has no money, so I don't think this was motivated by greed."

"Then what?"

"I wish I knew," Danita said.

"To help with your feeling of helplessness, you said you wanted to do something. What do you think your options are—other than interfering in a police investigation?"

"I'm not a detective. I'd have no idea where to start."

"Hmm. I suggest you focus on thinking cleansing and positive thoughts then."

Dr. Aminor was no help. "It's hard to do that when I'm so worried about her. I know what captivity can do to a person." Danita refused to think that her cousin was dead though. That negativity could prove deadly to her own soul.

"We talked about this. Negative thoughts are a feeding ground for your dark light to take over your body."

"I know." Damn Sanditra. Before the Royals had kidnapped her, Danita didn't have an ounce of dark light in her. After spending a few weeks with the very powerful witch, her white light had begun to dim. What she wouldn't give to be like her old self again.

"Understandably, you are angry and anxious," her therapist said, "but in your mental state, you might do something rash that could make things worse. What if Wendy's kidnappers took you too?"

She shrugged. "I'd at least be with Wendy."

"Danita."

She held up her hands. "Fine. I'll let the police handle things." For now. Besides, Griffin said he would look into it.

"Good. This week I want you to focus only on positive thinking. With a clear head, you might be able to figure out a way to help your cousin."

She doubted that, but it was worth a try. Danita stood, not any calmer than before she walked in, but after her Royal incarceration, she had promised Griffin she'd attend therapy. Just when she thought she was ready to embrace the world, her cousin was kidnapped, and Danita was attacked. Not doubt about it—she was cursed. "Thanks, Doc."

In need of a caffeine hit and a snack, Danita decided to walk over to Angelique's café instead of driving there. After being cooped up in that office for an hour, she needed the space and fresh air, though it wasn't as cathartic as she'd hoped. Horns made more noise than usual, people seemed pushier, and the wind was whipping her hair into her face and annoying her. For a moment, she was tempted to slow down the world around her to help calm her mind.

But she wouldn't use her magic in that way. While it only took a sweep of a hand and a silent chant, it would take more energy than she possessed right now. It also wouldn't be of any benefit to anyone. Using her powers for her own personal gain would only serve to foster her darkness, which was the last thing she wanted or needed. Ugh.

As soon as she entered the coffee shop though, her negative vibes diminished. Angelique, the restaurant owner, possessed a very powerful white light aura that affected everyone who entered. Her coffee shop was safe, giving Danita a small sense of control.

After ordering a drink and a snack, she snagged a table near the back, needing peace and quiet to think about her next move—a move that Dr. Aminor might not approve of.

HIDDEN REALMS OF SILVER LAKE (Paranormal)

Awakened By Flames (book 1)—FREE

Seduced By Flames (book 2)

Kissed By Flames (book 3)

Destiny In Flames (book 4)

Hidden Realms Box Set (books 1-4)

Passionate Flames (book 5)

Ignited By Flames(book 6)

FOUR SISTERS OF FATE: HIDDEN REALMS OF SILVER LAKE (Paranormal)

Poppy (book 1)

Primrose (book 2)

Acacia (book 3)

Magnolia (book 4)

Box Set (books 1-4)

WERES AND WITCHES OF SILVER LAKE (Paranormal)

A Magical Shift (book 1)

Catching Her Bear (book 2)

Surge of Magic (book 3)

The Bear's Forbidden Wolf (book 4)

Box Set(books 1-4)

Her Reluctant Bear (book 5)

Freeing His Tiger (book 6)

Protecting His Wolf (book 7)

Waking Her Bear (book 8)

Box Set (books 5-8)

Melting Her Wolf's Heart (book 9)

Her Wolf's Guarded Heart (book 10)

His Rogue Bear (book 11)

PACK WARS (Paranormal)—**BUY OR READ ON KU**

Training Their Mate (book 1)—FREE

Claiming Their Mate (book 2)

Rescuing Their Virgin Mate (book 3)

Box Set (books 1-3)

Loving Their Vixen Mate (book 4)

Fighting For Their Mate (book 5)

Enticing Their Mate (book 6)

Box Set (books 1-4)

Complete Box Set (books 1-6)

HIDDEN HILLS SHIFTERS (Paranormal)

An Unexpected Diversion (book 1)-FREE

Bare Instincts (book 2)

Shifting Destinies (book 3)

Box Set (books 1-3)

Embracing Fate (book 4)

Promises Unbroken (book 5)

Bear 'N Dirty (book 6)

Hidden Hills Shifters Complete Box Set (books1-6)

MONTANA PROMISES (Full length contemporary)—**BUY OR READ ON KU**

Promises of Mercy (book 1)

Foundations For Three (book 2)

Montana Fire (book 3)

Montana Promises Box Set (books 1-3)

Hart To Hart (Book 4)

Burning Seduction (Book 5)

Montana Promises Complete Box Set (books 1-5)

ROCK HARD, MONTANA (contemporary novellas)

Montana Desire (book 1)

Awakening Passions (book 2)

PLEDGED TO PROTECT (contemporary romantic suspense)—
BUY OR READ ON KU

From Panic To Passion (book 1)

From Danger To Desire (book 2)

From Terror To Temptation (book 3)

Pledged To Protect Box Set (books 1-3)

BURIED SERIES (contemporary romantic suspense)—**BUY OR
READ ON KU**

Buried Alive (book 1)

Buried Secrets (book 2)

Buried Deep (book 3)

The Buried Series Complete Box Set (books 1-3)

A NASH MYSTERY (Contemporary)—**BUY OR READ ON KU**

Sidearms and Silk(book 1)

Black Ops and Lingerie(book 2)

A Nash Mystery Box Set (books 1-2)

STARTER SETS

Contemporary—**BUY OR READ ON KU**

Paranormal

STANDALONES

A Billionaire's Roar

Author Bio

Want a FREE book? Sign up for my newsletter and receive free books.
COPY AND PASTE INTO YOUR BROWSER:
https://app.mailerlite.com/webforms/landing/i1e8b2

Check out my latest interview on You Tube:
http://youtube.com/sQo5pyyVMDI

Not only do I love to read, write, and dream, I'm an extrovert. I enjoy being around people and am always trying to understand what makes them tick. Not only must my books have a happily ever after, I need characters I can relate to. My men are wonderful, dynamic, smart, strong, and the best lovers in the world (of course).

I believe I am the luckiest woman. I do what I love and I have a wonderful, supportive husband, who happens to be hot!

Fun facts about me

(1) I'm a math nerd who loves spreadsheets. Give me numbers and I'll find a pattern.
(2) I love photography, so I'll be posting pictures—especially of my Costa Rican adventure.
(3) I also like to exercise. Yes, I know I'm odd. Not only do I lift weights, I love to hike and walk on the beach (yes, it sounds like an ad for a date)

I love hearing from readers either on FB or via email (hint, hint).

Social Media Sites

Website:
www.velladay.com

FB:
facebook.com/vella.day.90

Twitter:
@velladay4

Gmail:
velladayauthor@gmail.com

Google:
plus.google.com/u/0/116041077486216602121/posts

Instagram:
@dayvella

www.ingramcontent.com/pod-product-compliance
Lightning Source LLC
Chambersburg PA
CBHW050836180626
46814CB00007B/2490

* 9 7 8 1 9 4 1 8 3 5 9 5 1 *